AF485337

LOVE ME LONG TIME

A STANDALONE NOVEL

R.S. NICOLE

Love Me Long Time

Copyright © 2019 by R.S. Nicole
Published by Grand Pens Publications
grandpenz.com

All rights reserved. No part of this book may be used or reproduced in any form or by any means electronic or mechanical, including photocopying, recording, or by an information storage and retrieval system, without the written permission from the publisher and writer, except brief quotes used in reviews.

This is a work of fiction. Any references or similarities to actual events, real people, living or dead, or to the real locals intended to give the novel a sense of reality. Any similarity in other names, characters, places, and incidents are entirely coincidental.

SUBSCRIBE

Text Grand to 31996 to stay up to date with new releases, sneak peeks, contest, reading groups and more....

SUBMISSIONS

To submit your manuscript to Grand Penz Publications,
please send the first three chapters and synopsis to
grandpenzpublications@gmail.com

SYNOPSIS

Averi has always been a go-getter. Even coming from a family who has spoiled her since birth, she has always hustled for what she wanted, and didn't stop until she got it. At twenty-three, she is one of the most favored personal trainers in Miami, Florida, her business growing everyday. And nothing is better than having both her best friend Lacey and boyfriend, Josiah right by her side. But when Averi and Josiah's relationship starts to go downhill, Averi puts more of her focus into her work, which causes her to constantly bump into her first love, Tremaine Jackson.

Tremaine. Born and raised in Miami, Florida has always had hustling in his blood. After his sports bar became one of the hottest out, he wasted no time working on a new one. Tremaine feels like he is in a great spot in his life, the only problem is his up and down relationship with his girlfriend, Latoya. And running into his old highschool sweetheart Averi, didn't help his case. With these two constantly running into each other and both of their relationships on the outs, will they spark up an old flame?

Josiah is Averi's boyfriend of two years. While he

believes their relationship is picture perfect, Averi has other thoughts. With him losing his job and slouching around all day, Averi's tired and wants a change. Josiah loves Averi, but only for one thing. He knows he can't lose her, so he does the unthinkable, vowing to change his ways. But does change really last when you get a boyfriend who is only with you for what you have and what you can do for him?

Latoya is the definition of a gold-digger. Anything she wants, she gets it; but only from a man who is providing. Being in a relationship with Tremaine has a lot of perks and she would be a fool to lose her position in his life or giving her spot to the next chick. She gets noticed around town, has all of the latest, and she doesn't have to do much to get it. She's living in lavish. But as Tremaine starts to notice a change in her behavior, she slowly starts to get cut off and it doesn't make her happy. Being backed into a corner makes her do something she winds up regretting in the long run and when her secrets threaten her relationship, she isn't sure what to do.

ONE

AVERI

"Josiah!" I yelled as soon as I got done walking through the house. He didn't answer me, so I walked toward our bedroom. I could not believe the way this house looked. Here I am at work all day, and I have to come back home to a pigsty.

Once I walked in the room, of course he was laid across the bed knocked the hell out. Rolling my eyes, I yelled again. "Josiah! Wake the hell up!" He stirred a little in his sleep, but a smack to his face woke him up.

"Yo! What the fu–" he started, jumping up. "Keep your

hands to yourself Averi forreal. The fuck are you hittin' me for?"

"Because you wouldn't get your lazy ass up. Why is the house looking like this Jo? I asked you to clean up the messes you made this morning before I left for work, but it looks worse than it did earlier. The laundry is still overflowing, the kitchen is a hot ass mess, and the living room looks like a tornado came through. Like what the fu–" I stressed. "Never mind."

I didn't even like to yell, but he had me pissed. I was tired and sore as hell. All I wanted to do was come home, eat, and soak in the tub. Couldn't even do that.

"Look, I smoked a little earlier and it knocked me out. I'm sorry though babe. I got you tomorrow," he said nonchalantly. He tried to lean in for a kiss but I backed away. "Why you trippin'?"

"All this," I said, waving my hands around. "All this is why I'm tripping Jo. The house is a mess and with you here all day, it shouldn't be like this. I asked you before I left if you could do the laundry and clean the messes that you made up, but you can't even do that. I just left work and I have to come home to do more. I'm tired as fuck Jo."

Finishing my statement with finality, I walked over to the closet to change into some comfortable clothes so I could clean. I was getting tired of doing this. Jo tried to walk up and hug me from behind, but I snatched out of his embrace.

"Forreal Jo, leave me alone right now," I said. Then I walked out of the room so I could get started.

An hour and a half later, the house was spotless and the laundry was drying. It was a shame I had to do all of this by myself. I ended up calling my best friend Lacey, to see if she wanted to go get a drink or something to eat. Anything to get me out of this house. She agreed, so I went to go get a shower and get dressed.

I put on a simple white tight-fitted tank, a pair of ripped jeans, and Air Max's on my feet. My hair was just going to have to be in a messy bun because I damn sure didn't feel like doing it. Applying lip gloss to my lips, I was ready to be on my way.

"Where you going?" Josiah asked as I was walking out the door. "And what's for dinner?" he added.

"I'm going out and you can figure it out yourself, since I cleaned the house by myself. I'll be back later."

And then I walked out, making sure to slam the door shut behind me. I hit the button to unlock my car doors and then I slid into the driver's seat. I hit the steering wheel out of frustration and then put my head down. I didn't know how much more of this shit with Josiah I could take. If it wasn't enough that he was out of a job right now, being without one was making him lazy as hell. I know relationships are not always 50/50 and sometimes you will have to pick up what your partner is lacking, but I am tired.

Josiah got let go from his job a few months ago for failing a drug test and he has not found another one yet. Mostly because he wasn't looking. I was mad at first because it was his fault he lost the job, but then I played the role of the supportive girlfriend and gave him a little time to bounce back from the loss he took. Weeks turned into months and I was getting fed up with how lazy he got. He was a little lazy before, but being home all day turned him into a slob.

This situation was going to stress me out so instead of moping, I cut the music up and drove to meet Lacey. We decided to try this new sports bar called T.J's. It wasn't too far from my house and I've been wanting to go for a little while. I called Lacey and she said she was already seated which was perfect because I really wasn't in the mood to wait.

"So what's going on?" she asked as soon as I slid into the booth. One thing about Lacey, she could read me like a book. I knew her since middle school and she was like the sister I always wanted. Every time something was bothering me, she knew, always.

"Josiah," I said with a roll of my eyes. "Ever since he lost that job and he's been home all day, he's got so damn lazy. I came home today and the place was a mess. Oh and of course I was the one to clean it myself. I don't know how much more I can take Lace." The waiter came by and took our order for drinks, then Lacey spoke up.

"I say he's had enough time to sit on his ass and relax, give him an ultimatum. If he can't put up, he can get put out, boyfriend or not. I know you love him, but you shouldn't be doing everything by yourself. We all know you can afford it on your own, but there's no way a grown ass man should be living in lavish, doing what he wants and not putting shit towards the bills. We're not talking a couple of weeks Averi' it's been some months. Something's gotta give."

"You're right. I just don't want to argue about it all day and night."

"An argument shouldn't start from you expressing how you feel about something. If he can't handle a conversation about how you feel, he just doesn't give a damn."

I nodded my head and took in what she said. I did not want to believe that he didn't care, but his actions didn't show me differently. I excused myself to go to the bathroom and told Lacey to order me a hot wing platter with extra fries when the waitress came back. On my way back to the bathroom, I bumped into someone not even paying attention.

"Sorry, I wasn't even looking at where I was going," I said, still not looking up. But when I did, I looked into the most beautiful brown eyes. "Tremaine?" I said.

"Averi," he said, giving me a hug. "I didn't even know that was your short ass. What's been good with you?" I looked him over and had to admit he still looked good, as hell.

I met Tre or Tremaine in high school and we hit it off pretty good. I lost my virginity to him and everything. When we were dating, I even swore I was going to marry him one day. He broke my heart, though, the day I found out he cheated on me with a popular girl by the name of Latoya. I held the longest grudge against him over that bull. I was way past it now, but damn if being in his presence didn't bring back those memories.

"I'm good. Just here with Lacey trying this place out. I see you're dressed up though; what's the occasion?" I asked.

I was used to seeing him wear Polo, Gucci, and all of that. His pants sagging, with a cap on and gold fronts in his mouth. He looked like a straight businessman standing in front of me and he was damn sure wearing the hell out of the look.

"I just came from a meeting not too long ago. Just came back here to check on the place. This is my bar baby, I own it."

To say I was shocked was an understatement. I mean, Tre was smart as hell back in high school, but he didn't take it as serious as he should have. He was always skipping or showing up just to show off in a new outfit or something. I never even thought I would see him again, but I was happy I did and I was proud of what he had accomplished.

"Wow look at you. I'm proud of you," I said, playfully pushing his shoulder.

"Somethin' light. I'm actually working on opening another one. But I know you were probably headed to the bathroom and I need to fill out some paperwork. Mind if I get ya number?" he asked. And I got a little tingle in my belly. He was an old friend so I felt like it wouldn't be any harm, but I still felt a little funny about it since we were once together and I was with Josiah now.

"I actually have a boyfriend now, so I don't know about that one."

"I got a situation too. Nothin' wrong with old friends catching up though. Look," he said, taking a card out of his suit pocket and handing it to me.

"My number is on that card, both business and personal. I want you to use it. Oh and tell Lace I said wassup." Then he walked off, leaving me speechless. I went to go handle myself in the bathroom and then I went back to the table with Lacey.

"Well damn it took you long enough. Lucky the food didn't get here yet. You had to do a number two or something?"

"No damn," I said slightly embarrassed. She was always so loud. "I actually bumped into Tremaine on the way to the bathroom. We exchanged a few words and he gave me his number."

"What?!? He still look good?" she asked, still loud as hell. "And I would use that shit if I were you," she said, sipping her drink.

"Yes, still fine. He told me to tell you what's up, by the way." I definitely avoided her last comment which I'm sure she would catch on to.

"Your little proper ass," she said laughing. "Knowing

damn well he didn't say it like that. And don't think you're slick either, ignoring my comment and shit. You'll use the card, though. I already know it," she added.

The waitress came back with our food right after she said that and I was glad. I didn't want to go back and forth about this. Mainly because I didn't want her to be right. If I did use his number, it would just be old friends catching up like he said. No harm in that, right?

TWO
TREMAINE

Damn, Averi still looked good, and I mean good. Seeing her made me revisit high school days and I wondered if she thought about me in that way. I hated the way I did her, but I was young and dumb back then, thinking with the wrong head. I hoped she would use my number though, just so we could catch up a little.

I was in my office filling out some paperwork when my phone vibrated. *Where are you?* The text read. It was from my girl. Sighing, I sent a text back. *Where I said I would be.*

Why? She took forever to text back as always and it annoyed the shit out of me. Can't ask a question and take years to send something back.

I want to use your car. I'm going to Diva's house and I want those girls to hate off what I have, was her simple ass reply. I didn't even respond. Toya was on some other shit. Yeah, Toya is the Latoya that I was fooling around with back in high school. I don't even know how we made it this far without me choking the life out of her, but here we are. Everything was cool with us when we first started this, but over time, we have had some ups and downs. We were still going strong though.

Toya was always spoiled, so when I was working a job and not making that much, I wasn't surprised when she caught attitudes about not being able to depend on me to get stuff for her. What I didn't expect was for her to go out and cheat on a nigga, though; it actually broke me. I stopped going to work over that and eventually lost my job, so I ended up moving back in with my mom to get my shit back together.

She helped me get into school so I could do something with myself. I got my degree and that's when I started working on the sports bar I own now. I was bringing in so much money and business now, it was crazy. And I couldn't thank anyone but God and my ma dukes. She was so proud of me and that was all that mattered to me. A couple months after T.J's opened, Toya hit me up and said she wanted to talk. We had a long conversation and I still had love for her, so I told her we could work on us. I still had a little bit of trust issues with her though.

It was cool when we got back together, but as of lately, I wasn't feeling her attitude. This Toya, I wasn't used to; she was ten times worse. She was out here thinking we were famous or some shit. Trying to go to the fanciest restaurants, all the expensive stores, and trying to show off for people she considered her *friends*. None of that shit was me and I didn't want it to be her either, especially because money was coming in.

I loved having money, but I would never let it change me. I would step out of my comfort zone every once in a while, but I would never change who I am because there was some money in my pocket. A pack of Ramen noodles was going to be cooked before I went out for a steak at Ruth's Chris just because that was me. Toya didn't like that about me, but it wasn't my problem. We would talk about this new behavior though.

I walked out of my office after I finished up, in hopes that Averi was still here so I could see her before I left. I was bummed when I didn't see her, but I was damn sure hoping tonight wasn't my last time. I headed out the door after I checked on my staff, then I left them to it for the evening.

When I pulled up to the crib, every light was on and I got mad as fuck. I told Toya about this shit a million times and she acted like money grew on the trees sitting outside.

"Toya!" I yelled when I got in. She walked around the corner from being in the kitchen.

"I am right here T.J., damn. Why are you yelling?" I looked at her with my head cocked to the side. There was no way she didn't know what my problem was.

"Every light in this house is on, I done told you about that. If you're down here, there's no reason I see lights on upstairs."

"I forgot to turn them off. I was looking for my charger in the room. I had to pee and I just got a snack out the kitchen. I'm watching T.V. in here; it's no big deal. Just turn them off."

"Why can't you turn them off when you walk out a room? It's not that hard T."

I walked off and ended up turning the lights out anyway. There was no point in even trying to keep telling her about it. It was just going in one ear and out the other. She would end up doing the shit again, so I was done wasting my breath. After I turned the light in the hall out, I went to get a shower.

I don't know why but Averi was heavily on my mind while I was in here. I don't know if it was because I hadn't seen her in years or because she looked that damn good today. My mom never failed to let me know that she thinks of Averi as the girl who got away, but I was with Toya now and she would have to get used to that. I was definitely going to tell my mom I seen Averi though; she loves her as if she came out of her womb.

When I stepped out the bathroom, Toya was getting dressed. "I want to talk to you real quick before you leave," I said.

"It's gonna have to wait Tre. Diva called and said she wants to go out. Her brother just came home and she wants to celebrate at the club."

"So, she can't wait? I need to talk to you about some shit."

"Damn, can't you?" she sassed back. "We live in the same house. I'm sure you can wait until I get back. I'm gonna finish getting dressed at her house 'cause you're not gonna make me sweat my hair out. I'll be back later." She tried to kiss me, but I dodged it.

I didn't say anything else to her either. This is the type of shit I was getting tired of. She always had to go out somewhere, instead of sitting her ass down. I can't even come home from a long day to a home-cooked meal or an attentive girlfriend. I huffed, but eventually made myself something to eat and got comfortable. Another Friday night alone I guess.

THREE
AVERI

Ever since I left Josiah's ass at the house the other day, he has been walking around here ignoring me. It was childish as hell and I was putting a stop to it today. How is he walking around ignoring me when he's the one not doing anything all day is beyond me, but I was about to put an end to that too. Lacey is right. Jo is a grown ass man, and I have been playing the role of the supportive girlfriend for too long. He is going to have to make something happen and soon.

Walking downstairs, I thought Jo was going to be laying

on the couch, but the smell coming from the kitchen told me otherwise. When I walked in, Josiah was standing over the stove flipping pancakes. And it smelled good as hell in here. I hoped he didn't think this would be a peace offering though. We needed to have a serious talk and I prayed it didn't turn into an argument.

Making my presence known at the perfect time, Josiah turned to put the last pancake in the pan on one of the plates that sat on the island.

"Good morning baby. I was just about to come upstairs and get you," he said. He walked over to the fridge to get the juice out and then he placed two plates on the table along with silverware. "Did you want everything up here?" he asked me. Nodding my head, he began to make my plate.

I was actually sitting at the table in awe. I can't remember the last time Jo cooked me a meal, hell, even catered to me. I was definitely going to enjoy it though, but I wasn't going to let this nice gesture steer me away from the real issue. Making his way over to me, he placed my plate of eggs, bacon, sausage, pancakes and a bowl of fruit in front of me. Once he sat down across from me, we said grace and dug in.

Sipping my orange juice, I started speaking. "Jo, we really need to talk." I didn't like the look on his face, but I wanted to get this conversation out of the way sooner than later.

"I know and I'm sorry I've been acting like an ass lately. You don't deserve any of that and truthfully, I don't even deserve you and what you've been doing for me. You stuck by me and still are sticking by me through one of the worst times in my life and I know I haven't shown my appreciation for it, but just know that I do appreciate you baby." I was about to speak, but he started again.

"I love you and I'm sorry. I put my pride to the side in asking for handouts and I have an interview at one of the companies my uncle owns. He told me the job is mine but I told him I would still go and work to get it," he confessed, making me smile. "I promise shit is gonna change around here; that's my word and I'll show you."

He left me speechless, and I was hoping he was serious. I didn't want to keep arguing about and going through the same old motion. I wanted to be able to come home and not have to do more work, including taking care of a grown ass man. I loved Josiah to death, but I wasn't going to keep putting up with what was going on.

"I appreciate the apology Jo and I'm proud of you for making that step. I just don't want to keep going through this. I don't mind being supportive and being there for you, but I feel like I'm by myself in all of this Jo." I tried to hold back my tears, but they escaped my eyes anyway. I didn't want to cry, but the stress was really getting to me.

Getting out of his seat, he walked over to me and knelt down in front of me. "I'm sorry baby," he said, kissing my cheek. "You're not alone, and I'm sorry for making you feel like you are. I'm gonna get my shit together, I promise. Not only for me, but for you too. I got us." He rose from his spot on the floor and gathered the dishes to put them in the sink. I was about to get up to get a shower before I headed into the gym, but he grabbed my arm, pulling me back to him.

Picking me up, he started walking toward the island and put me down, my legs hanging off the edge. Standing in between my legs, he said, "I love you, Averi, and I'm sorry." I nodded and before I could tell him I loved him too, his lips crashed into mine while he guided my shorts down my legs. Our heads switching side to side, our lips locked and we sat in the kitchen kissing like two high school sweethearts. I was so into kissing him that I didn't even realize he was inside of me until he hit my spot.

"I love you Averi," he repeated, never missing a beat. All I could do again was nod my head. I can't remember the last time I felt like this while we were having sex, and I wanted to take full advantage of the moment. Reaching up and putting my hand on the back of his head, I pulled his head in closer, deepening our kiss. I know he loved when I did that because his strokes got deeper and a little while later, he released inside of me.

Catching our breaths, we shared one last kiss before Josiah pulled me from the island, my legs wrapping around his waist. He kissed my cheek before he put me down and then went to pick my shorts up for me. And I was glad he did that. My legs were definitely done for, and I didn't know how I was going to get through work today, but I really didn't have a choice.

FOUR

TREMAINE

Turning over and slamming my hand down on the alarm, I rolled over to Latoya's loud ass snoring, her mouth hanging wide open. I don't know why I was so irritated, but I was. Not letting it bother me though, I grabbed my phone off the table next to the bed and went to the bathroom so I could handle my morning hygiene.

After I wiped my face dry and finished putting on some cream, I checked my lock screen for notifications and got pissed instantly. Aside from all the emails, I seen about a million messages from my bank telling me how many times my card was swiped last night. Latoya done spent well over two thousand dollars in one night at one damn club, and I was pissed. It wasn't all about the money because I had plenty put away and brought in a lot, but it was about spending unnecessary money at a damn nightclub.

Walking out the bathroom, I snatched the covers back and yelled for her to get up. She turned over pissed but I gave no fucks at the moment; she would just have to be mad.

"You wanna tell me why you spent over two thousand at the club last night? Using my damn card," I said, frustrated. The way she just laid there all nonchalant about the shit had me hot, but I was trying to keep my frustrations under control.

Rolling her eyes, she sat up and started speaking. "It's not that serious T.J. damn. You act like you don't have the money. I took your card because I misplaced mine and I meant to ask you for another one."

"It's not about me having the money, Toya. You don't need to be out spending that shit at a raggedy ass nightclub. Do something useful with the money sometimes, damn. Didn't you say you wanted to get into cooking school?" I asked.

"Yeah but I changed my mind. You know how to cook so there's no point in me going. Look Tre, I'm sorry alright. But you have the money, stop acting like you're a broke ass dude because you're far from it. Now can I go back to sleep?" she had the nerve to ask. "I had a long night and I need my rest," she continued.

"Yeah of course you did." Walking over to the stand beside her, I snatched her purse up and dug around until I found my card.

"The fuck are you in my purse for Tre?!" she shouted,

jumping out the bed and snatching it up. If I didn't know any better, by the way she jumped up so fast, I would think she was hiding something. But if I needed to know something, I would definitely find out.

"Getting my fuckin' card. I'm out," I said with finality. The longer I stood in this room with her, the more pissed I was getting. And before I did anything I would most likely regret, I just left. Walking out the door and jumping into my ride, I headed in the direction of a new gym that was near the crib. I didn't feel like making the drive to my usual and I heard good reviews about this one.

When I pulled up, I hopped out my whip and walked in. It was clean as hell in here and I was happy I made the decision to come here. After I signed in as a guest until I decided if I wanted to be a member or not, I went to the locker room to put my shit away, then I walked back out to see the equipment. After checking out some of the machines, I knew what I needed to work on and I was ready to get it done.

Making my way over to one, I sat down ready to work on my arms and when I looked up, I seen Averi walk through the doors. And damn. I thought she looked good when she was at the bar not too long ago, but shit, seeing her in workout clothes did something to a nigga. I watched her go over to an empty room to set mats up, so I jogged over to see what she was up to.

"Avi-Ave," I said, calling her the name I gave her in high school. She was startled, but turned around and gave me a hug. And she smelled good as hell.

"Tre!" she yelled a little. "What are you doing at this gym?" she asked.

"Decided to come check it out. Needed to get away

from the crib and this gym was closer than the usual spot I go to, so here I am," I chuckled.

"Nice. You'll probably never go back to the other one, this gym is dope. Has everything you need really." I nodded my head.

"What are you settin' up in here big head?" I asked.

"For my class. I'm a personal trainer and I have classes four days a week. Personal sessions with clients who sign up for that on the weekends." And I smiled to myself.

"Damn, you always talked about that shit now look at you. I'm proud of you baby girl," I said. And I was. Ever since we met, she always talked about how she wanted to become a personal trainer and she made it happen. Her body always looked good, but shit, doing what she's doing made her look amazing.

"Thank you. It was rough at first, but I'm here," she said, showing her perfect smile. "Were you just here to work out or did you want to sign up for a class?"

"Work out a little bit, check out the machines. But what's your schedule like for these personal sessions? Could work somethin' out with that."

"On the weekends. I have an opening up for next weekend if you want to do that?" I agreed and then she wrote some stuff down in a little book and handed a card to me. "I know you gave me your number, but here's mine," she said, giving me her card.

"The class is going to start soon though, so I'll be texting you to remind you about the session okay?" I nodded again and left her to it. Taking one more glance in her direction, I smiled again at her doing what she loved. Walking over to the first machine, I got to doing my first workout.

. . .

FINISHING UP MY LAST SET, I looked over into the classroom and Averi looked like she was wrapping her class up. I jogged to the locker room to grab my stuff so I could catch her before she left. I wanted to take her somewhere for lunch and I wasn't going to take no for an answer either. I was sure she would like where we would be going too.

When she walked out, I ran over to her before she could walk out the door.

"Not so fast," I laughed. "Come with me. Let's go have lunch since it's early."

"I don't know about that Tre. I need to get home, shower, and do some things. And I'm sure my bo–" I cut her off there.

"Come on, just like old times. Please," I begged. And she knew I didn't do that shit for nobody else. Poking my bottom lip out, I was about to get down on my knees, but she laughed, stopping me.

"Alright," she said playfully pushing my shoulder. "I forgot you were a big ass baby." Laughing, she gathered up her things and we walked outside.

"I'll drive," I said. She looked at me skeptically, but I gave her a look that let her know she could trust me. Walking over to my truck, I took our things and tossed them in the back and jogged around to her side to open the door for her. Getting in the driver's seat, I sped out of the parking lot and we were on our way.

"So where are we going?" she asked. She was always nosey. Couldn't do anything without her asking a million questions.

"Can you just sit back and relax?" Looking over and seeing her face pout brought back some memories. It was so damn cute to me. Every time she did it, I would kiss her to make her smile. I knew I couldn't do that shit though and it bothered me a little bit, but we were both in situations and I would have to get over that.

Cutting the music up, I made my way over to my mom's house. I told my mom I ran into her and she has been begging me to bring her by. And I'm glad I ran into her today so I could make it happen.

When we got closer to my mom's, I told her to cover her eyes so she couldn't see anything.

"Why?" she asked. *There goes that nosey shit again.*

"Just trust me Averi, damn." She huffed, but then she did as I asked and relaxed a little. Getting out the car and walking over to her side to open the door, she stepped out and I covered her eyes, guiding her up the walkway. Reaching behind me to get my key, I unlocked the door and as soon as it opened, the smell of our favorite hit my nose.

"Oh my God, Tre. Tell me we're not at your mo–" she started, but the sound of my mom's voice cut her off.

"Averi!" she shouted loud as hell. And I never seen my mom move so fast in my life. She doesn't even come greet me like that.

"Aye, how come I don't get greeted like that and I'm your son?" I asked, my voice laced with jealousy.

"Because I see you almost every day," she sassed back. "You know Averi is my baby." She turned back to Averi. "Where have you been hiding girl?"

"Nowhere Ms. Leslie," she started. "I've been here. We just moved to the other side of Miami after I graduated and I fell out with everyone except Lacey. I've missed you though," she said, showing off that pretty smile again.

"Don't let that shit happen again," my mama said sternly.

"Yes ma'am," Averi replied, laughing her statement off.

"Now come eat some of this gumbo I made y'all. It's still your favorite?" she looked to Averi for an answer.

"Wouldn't want to eat gumbo anywhere else," she said, making my mom smile. Then we walked toward the kitchen.

My phone vibrated in my pocket for the hundredth time and when I pulled it out, it was Toya's ass once again. I still wasn't fucking with the shit she pulled and I wasn't about to let her kill my good mood. Turning my phone off and sliding it in my back pocket, I joined the ladies in the kitchen and we enjoyed the food my mom prepared.

Three bowls later, I was laid out on the couch, while Averi and my mom were on the other couch bonding like mother and daughter. I loved the sight and it was moments like this I wish I hadn't done Averi dirty. If I regretted anything in life, it was definitely that but I couldn't turn back. I was about to doze off, but the ringing of my mom's doorbell and the banging on the door stopped that from happening.

Jumping up, I instantly got defensive. I don't know who was bold enough to bang on the door and ring the doorbell out of control, but whoever it was, was about to get their ass handed to them. I told my mom and Averi I had it under control and walked toward the door. And as soon as I snatched it open, I was face to face with Latoya. *Fuck my life.*

FIVE
LATOYA

After Tre left with his little attitude this morning, I laid right back down and went to sleep. I don't know why he kept wasting his breath about stuff like that, he knew he was going to give me a new card to use and I was going to do the same thing. I was tired of him bitching about small things like that anyway. He had the damn money and spending two thousand wasn't putting a dent in his pockets, at all.

After some more much needed beauty sleep, I tried calling him so I could meet him somewhere and get some money. It had been a couple hours and I'm sure he was over his little attitude by now. The fact that he wasn't answering the phone was pissing me off. And when he didn't answer the tenth time I called, I took it upon myself to go to his usual spots. If he didn't want to answer me, I was going to pop up, simple.

I know the bar is his baby aside from me, so that's where I stopped first. I knew two of his little workers would give me any answer I was looking for as long as I flirted a little bit, but when they said he hasn't been in all morning, I got pissed. *This is the first place he usually stops even if it's for five damn minutes,* I thought. The next place I checked was the gym and I swear if he wasn't there, I was guaranteed to get pissed off.

Calling him, I still got no answer and I was livid. He even turned his phone off, which had me all the way hot. I knew one last place I could try and I was hoping to be in luck. Even though I didn't want to go over there, I was out of options and this was my last resort. Sighing, I put the directions to go to his mom's house in my GPS.

I know his mom doesn't like me, and the feeling is definitely mutual. She hasn't liked me since the first day Tre brought me around her, not that I care anyway. I'm not fucking her, so her opinion of me doesn't really matter. But the fact that Tre is a damn mama's boy irks my nerve. Whenever he goes over there, I stay home and I damn sure don't go over there by myself.

When I finally pulled onto her street, I saw his truck and instantly got pissed. I don't know why he had to turn his phone off being over here, but I was ready to find out. Hopping out of my car and slamming the door, I marched up the walkway and started banging on the door, ringing the bell at the same time. I knew whoever answered was going to be pissed but I didn't care. I was pissed Tre turned his phone off and he was going to know just how pissed I was.

The door finally swung open after what felt like forever and the face I was met with wasn't pleasant at all. Tre looked like he was ready to explode, but when I peeked around him and seen Averi sitting on the couch with his mom, I was ready to match his energy. I was so irritated that I did something I never thought I would do. Reaching my arm back, I was in the middle of bringing it around to slap the shit out of him, but the death grip he had on my wrist stopped me from doing so. And I regretted trying to hit him right after.

Tre's face looked even worse and his lips were so tight, I didn't think they could get any tighter. He was about to say something, but his mom jumping up from her spot on the couch stopped him from doing so.

"I know damn well you weren't about to put your hands on my son you little ghetto, bit–" she started, but was cut off by Tre.

"Ma, chill out," he said. "I got it." I thought he would say something about her disrespecting me, but I guess not.

"So you're just gonna let her talk to me like that Tremaine?" I asked, tears forming in my eyes. Usually I wouldn't even care, but seeing Averi's bougie ass sitting on the couch had me in my feelings and I still wanted to know what she was doing here. "And what is this bitch doing here?!" I yelled.

"Listen," Averi started. "You're mad at the wrong person. I'm here to see his mom, nothing more, nothing less. And I didn't disrespect you, so don't disrespect me." She got her bougie ass up from the couch and for a second I thought she was coming over to leave out, but she gave Tre's mom a hug.

"Sorry Ms. Leslie," she started. "Thank you for the meal, but I need to go. I'll be by to see you soon," she smiled. And I got irritated all over again. She was beautiful, couldn't even deny that. I hated her.

They hugged again and she was ready to walk out the door, but Tre stopped her.

"Where are you goin'?" he asked. And I looked at him sideways.

"I'm getting Lacey to pick me up so she can take me back to my car. I don't have time for this Tremaine. I'll see you later," she said before pushing past him. I stepped to the side so I could avoid provoking her any further. I had bark, but no bite. And Averi would whoop my ass out here for sure.

"Hold on Averi, just let me–" he started, but she cut him off.

"You're good Tre, I'll see you later." And then she started down the walkway and walked up the street. She stood at the corner for a good ten minutes before she made a left and then that was the last we saw of her. Taking a look at Tre, the mug was still plastered on his face. I tried to step closer to go in the house, but of course his mom had an objection.

"You know damn well you're not welcome in this house. Get your little ghetto ass off of my porch and don't bring that shit over here no more. And the next time you try to put your hands on my son, I'll beat your ass myself," she concluded. Pushing Tre out of the house, she slammed the door in both of our faces. Walking away, I got to the driver's side of my car. Looking up at Tre, he kept quiet, giving me the most hateful stare.

"Yo, what's your problem?" He finally spoke.

"My problem? What's yours? You're out here letting

both Averi and your mom disrespect me in front of your face like I'm not your damn girlfriend. And what the fuck was she over here for anyway?" I snapped.

"Lower your tone. I'm talking to you with respect, so I expect the same. And she told you what she was over here for; we don't need to go over that again." He ran his hands down his face, but continued. "Why are you over here anyway?" he had the nerve to ask. "You don't come over here any other time, not even when I ask," he added.

"I was looking for your ass," I snapped again. "What is your damn phone off for?"

"I didn't feel like dealing with this shit today Toya. I sent you a text and said I'm busy and I'll get back with you, but you kept callin'. So I cut my shit off," he said all nonchalant. "And I'm not gonna tell you again, talk to me like you got some sense or it can get real ugly out here."

"Anything could have happened to me Tremaine or do you not care about that?" I replied, hoping to get some kind of empathy out of him.

"You made it over here, you're fine." Tears formed in my eyes again and this time I let them fall. I don't know what was wrong with him today, but I didn't like this new attitude he had.

"Is it Averi?" I asked, afraid of the answer. "Is it because you ran into Averi?"

"What? No, cut it out. I'm not even about to do this right now." Moving closer to me, he grabbed my face and kissed my forehead.

"We'll talk about it later," he said with finality. Leaving me standing outside my car, he made his way over to his truck, jumped in and drove off.

Sliding into the driver's seat in defeat, I let the rest of my tears fall and then I wiped my face dry. I wasn't about to sit here and cry over this bullshit all day. Calling my girl Diva, I told her I was coming over and to have something ready for me. I would just spend a few hours over there. Tre could go home if he wanted to. I damn sure wasn't.

When I finally made it to her house, smoke filled the room as soon as I walked in and I was feeling better already. Taking a seat on the couch, I made myself comfortable and picked up the weed that was on the table. I was ready to ask where some blunts were, but I took a look to my left and Diva's brother, Jayshawn was coming down the stairs. And I couldn't help but react to him.

Jayshawn, or Jay, is Diva's older brother that just got out of jail and I swear if I wasn't with Tre, I would have been jumped at the chance to get with him. I didn't know what I was going to do about this situation with Tre, but I wasn't even going to worry about it right now. I had weed in front of me, a bottle on the way, and Diva's brother to keep me company.

"Wassup lil mama," he greeted. I shot a smile his way and he returned it, showing off his gold fronts.

"Not a thing. Where's your sister?"

"She went down the street to some raggedy hoe's house," he replied. *Lamisha,* I thought. "You smoke?"

"I know you see this weed in my hand," I sassily replied. "I'm trying to roll 'em." I seen him reach in his pocket and he handed me the wrapper. I took a blunt out and then prepared to roll it. After I was done, Jay looked in amazement.

"So you do know how to roll," he smirked. I tilted my head toward him letting him know I didn't play, then I lit it. We passed it back and forth until it was gone and then he rolled another one.

"I need something to drink now," I said. He looked at

me shocked, but again, I tilted my head. This is our first time really being alone and he was about to find out how I got down when I was with Diva.

"You playin' a dangerous game lil mama, but I got you," he said, getting up from the couch. He started walking toward the stairs which I found odd because the bar was in the back.

"Where are you going?" I asked out of curiosity.

"To the real liquor. You comin'?" I knew where we were about to go. Just didn't know if it was a good idea. But against my better judgment, I got my ass up and followed him up the stairs to his room.

GETTING TOSSED ON THE BED, I was positioned on all fours. I didn't even get a chance to move before Jay inserted me again.

"Oh my–" I tried to get out. Jayshawn was so deep, I couldn't even form my words. We had been at it for a little while and I hoped this was the last round. I don't know how much more I could take.

"Arch it," he demanded. Smacking my ass twice, he grabbed my hips and his strokes were even deeper than before. After he delivered a few more, he released himself inside of me and fell to the side. "You got some good shit," he complimented. And I smirked. I tried to get up but I had no energy and before I knew it, I laid back on the bed and dozed off.

When I woke up, I reached for my phone but remembered it was downstairs. Looking around, it was dark as hell so I knew it had to be late. Jumping up, I put my clothes back on and went down the hall to the bathroom. What I wasn't expecting was to run into Diva on the way there.

"When did you get back?" I asked embarrassed. I didn't know how much she heard and I really didn't want to hear her mouth about it.

"Been here for a little while." *Shit.* "But I don't care, y'all are grown. Just keep my brother out of your shit and make sure you know what you're doin'."

"I have it under control," I said. But I didn't know if I believed that shit myself.

"Alright. Just sayin'. Jay is possessive as fuck and since you went there, you won't get rid of him that easy," she shrugged. "The fuck did you drink anyway?" she laughed.

"Don't even ask," I said, putting my head down. "I gotta go though." Rushing past her, I took a little bath at the sink and got to my car as fast as I could. When I looked at the time, it was going on eleven. I didn't have any calls or texts from Tre which had me a little irritated, but relieved at the same time. I would just face him when I got home.

Pulling up, I didn't see his truck and it had me wondering where he was. I pulled my phone out of my purse and dialed him, but it went straight to voicemail. I was ready to call him back, but a text came through. *Staying at my mom's, I'll be at the crib tomorrow,* was his message. I just put my phone back in my bag. Going in the house, I went straight to the shower and got in bed. Him staying at his mom's house probably wasn't such a bad idea after all.

SIX

AVERI

Things at the house have been way different since Jo started working. I mean, he did a complete turnaround. I barely had to do anything around here. Before, I was doing the cleaning, all of the cooking, and buying, but Jo wouldn't let me do any of it as of lately. I was actually happy that we were getting back to the equality in our relationship. This *new* Jo is the man I missed seeing.

After getting out of the shower, I dressed in my workout clothes and made my way to the gym. Sometimes, I hated doing these personal sessions. I wanted my me time on the weekends, but I was making money so I couldn't do too much complaining.

Walking in the gym, the first person I saw was Tre, which surprised me. I know he had another gym he went to on a regular, but by the looks of it, he was done with that one. I was about to go to the class I did my sessions in, but Tre jogged over to me and stopped me from going inside.

"Can we talk?" he asked. I figured he would want to talk about the day at his mom's, but I wasn't trying to.

"What about?" I asked, trying to seem annoyed.

"My mom's house. I wanted to apologi–" I cut him off there.

"We're just friends remember?" I replied, mocking the last time he said that. "You don't owe me any explanation about that. We're good Tre." And as soon as I finished speaking, my client walked through the door ready to go. "I have to go," I added.

Walking away, I knew I didn't mean what I just said. Seeing Latoya at his mom's house actually made me feel some type of way. It just brought back old memories. I thought I was over what Tre did back in high school, but to know he was actually still with her, was a little upsetting. I thought he would have learned from his mistakes, but I guess he didn't. Putting that to the back of my mind, I got ready to work with my client.

A little over an hour later, the session was wrapped up and I was ready to go. I called Jo to let him know that I was ready to be picked up, since he wanted to drop me off today for whatever reason. Walking outside, I was sitting on the bench scrolling through my phone, when Tre sat down beside me, interrupting me.

"Got a minute?" he asked. I did, but I didn't want to make any time if he was going to try and apologize again.

"Yeah, what's up?"

"I just wanted to know if we were still on for the personal session next week. I took a few glances at you workin' and I need a few of those workouts." Staring into his eyes, I knew there was more he wanted to say, but he held it back.

"Yeah, Saturday?"

"That works." He was about to say something else, but Josiah pulling up put a damper in his plans.

Getting up and walking over to the car, Josiah jumped out and came around to open my door. I knew that was because Tre was sitting here because he didn't do this on a daily basis, but I was going to leave it alone. When he got back in the driver's seat he grabbed my face and kissed me, something else he didn't normally do.

Moving away from his embrace, I turned to put my seat-belt on, while taking one last look at Tre. He had a jealous look on his face but there was nothing I could do about that. I just put the seat back and enjoyed the ride.

"How was today's session bae?" Jo asked.

"It was alright, the usual. This client works really hard though. I admire his determination to lose the extra weight he put on. Why did you want to pick me up today?"

"Just because. So that was Tremaine from back in the day huh?"

"Why say it like that? But yeah it was him. Why?"

"I'm just askin' baby. Y'all be hangin' out or somethin'?" *I don't know where these questions are coming from, but I damn sure don't like them,* I thought.

"No, I ran into him the other day when I was coming for one of my classes and he's been coming here since. He scheduled a personal session but other than that, we don't talk," I truthfully admitted, purposely leaving out me going to his mom's house with him for lunch the other day.

"Oh aight, just makin' sure he still don't got any feelings. You're all mine and you're not goin' nowhere." He winked and I replied with a nervous chuckle.

Something about the way he said that didn't sit right with me, and I don't know where this talk came from all of a sudden, but I didn't like it. Jo never had a jealousy issue and he never had a worry of losing me. For him to mention that randomly, had me eyeing him sideways a little. But if I needed to know something, I would find out.

When we pulled up in front of our house, I noticed a black car with tinted windows parked across the street. I always took in my surroundings and I have never seen this car anywhere near the house since we have been living here, so I instantly got a bad feeling from it. When I told Jo, he looked over, but his facial expression didn't change. As soon as we got out of the car, the window to the black car rolled down and an arm reaching out signaled for Jo to walk over.

"Who is that Jo?" I asked curiously.

"Just somebody who works for my uncle bae. You have to relax. Go take a nice bath or somethin'. I'm gon' see what this nigga wants," he replied, giving me a kiss before he jogged across the street. I still had a bad feeling about it, but I took his word for it and went in the house.

Finally getting up to my room and getting settled, I called Lacey to fill her in about the events that just took place.

"Left with who?" she asked when I told her about Josiah and the random car.

"I don't know, but I don't have a good feeling about it," I admitted. "I'm coming over."

"Mmcht," she sucked her teeth. "Well I have some wine I've been wanting to drink; the door's open for when you get here." And that's why this girl is my best friend. Hanging up with her, I went to take a much needed bath to soak this soreness away.

Picking up my phone, there were no calls or texts from Jo, so I dialed his number to let him know where I would be. He didn't pick up, so I just sent a text. I was about to put my phone down, but a text coming through stopped me from doing so. *I still wanna talk to you, hit me back please.* Already knowing it was from Tre, I locked my phone and put it up, getting ready to make my way over to Lacey's house for our girl's night.

The week went by so fast and it was already the day of my personal session I had set with Tre. I haven't heard anything since the other day when he texted me and I was relieved. Josiah was acting more possessive these days and I did feel like it had something to do with Tre. Either way, Jo didn't have anything to worry about. Tre has Latoya and that's who his focus needs to be on.

Pulling up to the gym, I sat in the car for a few minutes to mentally prepare for this session with Tre. I wasn't nervous or anything, I just didn't want him to try and continue the conversation he was trying to have. What happened at his mom's happened already and it's just best that we all move on from it. Even though every time I did see him, memories from high school flooded my mind and some of them were not pleasant. Sighing, I exited my car and walked into the gym.

As soon as I finished setting up in the room, Tre walked in. I almost felt as if him wearing a tight muscle shirt showing off his perfectly toned body was on purpose, but I wasn't going to feed into it. When he walked in the room, he set his bag down and gave me the longest stare, but eventually turned his attention to the equipment that was set up.

"You really be doin' the damn thing," he said, starting off the conversation.

"I do," I replied. "Want to get started now? Or you need some time?"

"I was born ready baby," he said, winking. Walking to where he was, I stood beside him, and we got to work.

FINISHING up the last few minutes, Tre jumped up as soon as I yelled we were done. I never seen someone run over to get their water bottle so fast. He was drenched in so much sweat, I'm surprised he moved as quickly as he did.

"You good?" I asked, teasing.

"Hell yeah, I'm definitely gonna feel this one in the morning though," he replied. "I didn't know your shit was this hardcore."

"I do a little something," I sassed. "Setting up another one, or I'm too much?" I joked again.

"Hell nah," he laughed. "I'm straight. Just wanted to see how you get down. I'm good on workouts for a week," he laughed again. This time I joined.

"Well good, I won't have to see your big head ass coming in the gym anytime soon," I joked back.

"That you won't, but only if you come by the bar one of these days or back to my mom's," he added.

I had a skeptical look on my face and I'm sure he noticed because of what he said next. "Look Averi, I want to apologize for that shit at my mom's," he started. I was ready to cut him off again, but he didn't let me this time.

"I need to get this out. Averi look, I'm sorry about Latoya poppin' up at my mom's crib. She didn't have no business bein' there. Shit, she knows that she's not even welcome there. And I know it probably made you a little uncomfortable seeing her, especially with her showin' up, so I'm sorry," he finished.

"You really didn't have to apologize, but I appreciate it. Latoya's your woman, so I get why she came. Everything is okay though," I reassured. "But the next time she disrespects me, I might have to beat her ass," I laughed, but I was dead serious.

"I'm actually surprised you didn't," he laughed. "Your feisty ass would knock bitches out for looking at you wrong." We shared a laugh. Aside from us being together before, me and Tre were friends first and we did have a special bond. I wouldn't mind having that back.

There was a little silence after that, but Tre broke it by saying that he had to go. I was actually ready to go, too, so we walked out together and he pulled me in for a hug. It lasted a little long, so I pulled back and we smiled before we went our opposite ways. Getting in my car, I was ready to make my way home. After the little talk me and Tre just had, I actually had a good feeling about our friendship. I knew we would be able to get back to a good place soon.

When I finally made it home from the gym, I opened

the door and what was spread out in the living room, caught me by surprise. There was a giant teddy bear, flowers, a few gift bags on the floor, and a card on the couch. I didn't even know what to pick up first, but I ended up walking over to the couch to pick up the card. Opening the envelope and taking it out, it had instructions for me to follow and Josiah had the whole day planned out for me. I didn't know what he was up to, but I was actually anxious to see what he had up his sleeve.

After I took a shower, there was a large box on the bed that wasn't there before I got in. I skeptically walked over to it and when I lifted the top off, I laid my eyes on the most beautiful dress. Picking up the note beside the box, it was written by Josiah, letting me know to have it on by seven o'clock tonight. Now I was even more excited to see what was going on. Josiah never did anything surprising like this and it was making me anxious to find out.

FINALLY MAKING it back to the house, it was going on six, so I still had an hour to get ready. I couldn't believe everything Josiah had planned today. He made an appointment for me at a new spa and I got everything done, down to a much needed massage. And he made me a hair appointment. My hair was curled to perfection, flowing down my back. I was happy about not having to do it myself. After I slipped the dress on and strapped the heels, I looked up to see Jo walking in the room dressed in a matching tux.

"You look good boo," he complimented me. Walking over to me, he grabbed both sides of my face, bringing my lips to his. "If we didn't have somewhere to be, that dress would be coming off," he smirked. Spinning me around, he gave my butt a light tap, before he walked into the bathroom.

"Thanks babe, but what's all this for? Where are we going?" I asked, hoping he would tell me something.

"Why you gotta be so nosey?" he laughed. "I got everything under control. You ready?" I nodded my head and he walked over to me again, kissing my forehead. "Let's get it then," he concluded. Locking everything up, we walked outside hand-in-hand and there was a limousine out front waiting.

"Jo, what is this? How did you get a limo working with your unc–" I started, but was cut off.

"Averi, chill out," he said sternly. "You know my uncle's shops bring in a lot of money and he has several. He hit me off with a bonus for workin' hard and bringin' more business, that's all," he assured me, kissing my nose. "Do you trust me?" he asked.

"Yeah Jo, I do," I replied honestly. I did trust Jo, but something just seemed off. He is a hard worker though so I wouldn't be surprised if his uncle did do that for him. I would just push this to the back of my mind.

"Aight then. Ladies first," he said, extending his arm out so I could walk. The driver opened the door for me and then Jo got in right after.

Looking around, I was in awe. I'd never been in a limo before and my first time was a little better than what I expected. The decorations inside were beautiful, the soft music playing in the background was so nice, and there were bottles of champagne accompanied by little snacks.

"Jo this is perfect," I started. "Thank you." I kissed him, and then he poured us both a glass of champagne. Clinking glasses, we took a sip and then we pulled off.

When we came to a stop, I looked out the window and

we were at one of the most expensive restaurants in the city. Looking at Jo, he looked calm, while I was anxious on the inside. *First a limo and now an expensive restaurant. The hell is this man up to?*

The driver then opened his door to get out and then came around to get us. Jo stepped out first then extended his hand to me so that I could follow. I felt as if all eyes were on us and I didn't really like it. I was actually nervous as hell. But I put my poker face on as we walked toward the door. As soon as Jo opened it to let me walk in first, I seen both of our parents, plus Lacey sitting at a table. Looking at Jo, he avoided eye contact with me, as he should have. Getting to the table, I sat down in the chair that was next to Lacey and he sat beside me.

"Lace, what's going on?" I whispered.

"Hell if I know," she laughed. "You know I would rather be at home stuffing my face than be anywhere Josiah is," she replied back, louder than she needed to. Rolling my eyes, I paid attention to everyone else, greeting them. Soon, we had our food and drinks ordered, having good laughs and conversation, until Jo stood up to get everyone's attention.

Clinking his glass, he started speaking. "First, I would like to thank everyone for coming out to this dinner tonight. I appreciate every single person here, especially you, Averi," he said, turning toward me. "From the first day I met you, I knew I wanted to be with you, and that you were going to be mine."

Standing in front of me and kneeling down on one knee, he took my hand in his and said," Averi Marie Jordan, will you marry me?" Tears pooled into my eyes before he even got the question out and I was at a loss for words. I definitely wasn't expecting this.

"Averi, baby. My knee is starting to hurt," Josiah said,

letting out a small chuckle. "Will you m–" he attempted to get out again, but was cut off by me screaming yes.

As I jumped up, applauds came from everywhere in the restaurant, and tears flew down my face at a rapid pace. We kissed and shared a long hug, before Jo broke it apart, letting me know he had to use the bathroom. Wiping his tears, I kissed him one last time before I sat down, admiring my ring. Averi Martinez... I would be Mrs. Averi Martinez.

Stepping into the bathroom, I stood in front of the mirror for a few minutes, reflecting on the fake ass performance I put on back there. Splashing a little water on my face, I wiped it with one of the towels and smiled to myself. Pulling out my phone, I sent out a text. *It's done.* Slipping it back into my pocket, I smiled again.

I was actually surprised Averi said yes, but I was glad she did. I guess the little change I pulled was working. I loved Averi, I really did, but the money she had and brought in was the most attractive thing about her. I needed to lock her down, forever. Her business was growing each day and she was working on a new project she didn't think I knew about. Either way it went, she was locked in and so was her money.

I felt like I was in the bathroom too long, so before anyone got suspicious or worried, I washed my hands and left out. When I was nearing the table, I witnessed Averi admiring her ring, Lacey right beside her. She looked up at me and gave a hateful stare, but fixed her face as I got closer. Lacey always hated me for whatever reason, but unknowingly, she did have a valid one.

Sitting beside my wife-to-be, I kissed her cheek and whispered in her ear. "Ready to get out of here?" I asked. "The night isn't over yet." She looked skeptical like she usually did when she was surprised about something, but the look I gave her stopped her from asking anything else.

I had booked a room for the rest of the weekend in a hotel that Averi's been wanting to stay at since the beginning of our relationship. I hoped she didn't ask about the money being spent on anything. I did have a little something going on, but as long as that stayed just my business, everything would be alright. Wrapping the dinner up, everyone said their goodbyes and that left me and Averi to it.

When we pulled up to the hotel, I wish I could have captured the look on Averi's face, it was priceless. Her expression showed excitement, but I know she was more surprised than anything. She was about to speak, but I cut her off. "Tonight is about you, about us babe. No questions." Giving me a side eye, she nodded and just went along with it, like I hoped she would.

After checking in, we went up to the room and the reaction I got from Averi was just what I was expecting. She went straight over to the bed and took a picture of the roses I had set up, shaped into a heart that had our names and the day we got engaged in the middle. If she hadn't said yes to me, this whole night would've been a bust. That's part of the reason why I was happy she did.

Turning around in my direction, she slipped her heels off and raced over to me, jumping in my arms. "I love you Jo," she told me in that sweet little voice of hers. It almost made me feel bad, but I pushed that to the back of my mind to focus on this moment. "And I don't know what else to say except for this night has been perfect."

"Don't say anything," I whispered back to her. "Just enjoy tonight and the rest of the weekend." Kissing her nose, then her lips, I continued. "And I love you too baby." Setting her down, I kissed her deeply, my hands roaming her body, then resting on her lower back. Guiding her to the bed, I pushed her down and put my body on top of hers. And after only a few minutes inside of her, I knew this night would end on a good note.

NINE

LACEY

When Josiah first came to me about going to a restaurant, I didn't know what to think but then when he started inviting everyone, I figured he was up to something. What I didn't expect was for him to propose to Averi. I mean I was happy for my friend, she deserves all of the happiness coming her way. But I just feel like she's with the wrong person. Something about Josiah doesn't sit right with me, but in due time I would figure it out.

I never really cared for him. Something always bothered me when it came to him and I always expressed it to Averi, which is why she barely mentions him when she's around me. And not to mention that just not too long ago, he was being a leech. But if Averi liked it, I loved it. I just wish she would open her eyes and realize she belongs with Tremaine.

I hated how he did her back in high school but for some reason, I know those two were made for each other. They can be with whoever they are with all they want to, but I know they belong together and I can't wait for them to see it. For now, I would play the role of the supportive best friend and not bring any of this up to her. I just hoped she would come to her senses. Josiah isn't for her, and I needed her to see that.

Aside from Averi and her drama, I had a lot going for myself. Even though Averi was younger than me by a year and some months, she inspired and motivated me every day. When she pursued her passion with personal training, she inspired me to get into my fashion designs and also working on my nails. So that's what I've been doing in my spare time. I was also helping Averi design her new line of workout clothes and it was nice to combine our talents and come up with something.

I was actually on my way to meet Averi at a space that is available. The location wasn't the biggest or in the best spot, but it could be mine and that's all I have ever wanted. When I parked my car, I was about to get out, but I saw Latoya walking beside some guy and it definitely wasn't her man. I didn't want to jump to any conclusions. Maybe it was a relative or something, but it didn't seem right. Either way, Averi was going to hear about it.

After a few minutes, Averi pulled into a spot that was two over from mine. When I got out to meet her, she had a mug on her face.

"What's wrong with you?" I asked.

"Josiah," she said, rolling her eyes. And I returned the favor. "We argued before I left the house over Tre's ass. Like you just proposed and now you're being insecure. I'm wondering if that's the reason he did it," she said, sadness present in her tone.

Popping her in the back of the head, I said, "I know you're fuckin' lying. Don't even go there. He proposed because you're it Averi and I mean *it*. You have everything a man needs and he proposed because he loves you. Shit, to be honest, he doesn't even deserve you," I ranted, making sure I said the last part under my breath.

We've had so many arguments about her and Josiah, it made no sense and I wasn't trying to have another one. It was a good day, and I was in a good mood. I needed it to stay that way. Averi sighed, but switched her energy and we got ready to look at the place.

I took one last look over to where I seen Latoya and her *friend,* and when I witnessed them kiss, I knew then she was out doing dirt. And in due time, Tre would find out just how dirty this broad is and has always been.

TEN
TREMAINE

It's been a few weeks and over this time, I've been working on the second bar that I want to open. Everything was going steady and I was ready for it to open. The inside was almost done and then I would order the furniture. After that, I would hire some people and my second business would be up and running.

Aside from working, I've been in the gym a lot more all while avoiding the mess out of Averi. I went to see my mom the other day and when she broke the news that Averi was engaged, I damn near passed out. To say I was upset when I heard that was a damn understatement and I know my mom felt my pain because she made me my favorite dish of hers, but that only fixed part of how I was feeling. The only thing that distracted me was working and working out, which was what I was on my way to do now.

Pulling up to the gym, I felt a knot form in the pit of my stomach, but I was going to go in anyway. I knew I couldn't avoid Averi forever and since I made this gym my permanent spot, I would have to face her sooner or later. When I walked out of the locker room, I seen Averi bending down to tie one of her shoes and the first thing I noticed was the ring on her finger. It wasn't anything special, but she had it on, so she must have been proud to wear it.

Getting up from her stance, she turned toward me and we locked eyes. I wanted to say something, but I chose not to and broke the stare to do my first workout. Running on the treadmill, I knew I couldn't keep lying to myself about how I feel when it comes to Averi. I never stopped loving or thinking about her, but her moving on and me being with Latoya ruined any chance of me getting her back. And now her man was standing in the way of me expressing my true feelings to her. Latoya was too in a way, but I think our time to end this relationship has come.

Shit isn't and hasn't been the same for a while between us. After I took her back, things were smooth. But deep down inside, I knew I would never trust her the same again and without trust, there's nothing. Besides, all we've been doing lately is arguing and that's another reason I've just been working all the time. I would get up early in the morning and come back late at night, just to avoid arguing with her ass. I was getting tired of the bullshit and I was gonna put an end to it soon.

Finishing up, I seen Averi getting ready to leave. I

wanted so badly to walk over there and say something to her, but I opted out of it. I would just hit her up about another session soon. Hopping in my truck, I started it up and drove off. I didn't know how I wanted to start this conversation off with Toya when I got home, but I knew it needed to happen today. I couldn't keep lying to myself about how I felt. It's not fair to Toya and it's damn sure not fair to me.

When I got in the house, the lights to the rooms that aren't being occupied were off to my surprise. Even though Latoya's car was outside, I was wondering if she was even home it was so dark and quiet. Getting up to our room, I threw my bag down and was on my way to take a much needed piss so I could get this conversation out of the way, but I heard Toya sick in the bathroom. Rushing in there, I sat on the side of her, holding her hair back. It smelled horrible and as much as I wanted to get up and let her be, a part of me wouldn't do that. I knew I couldn't say what I wanted while she was like this either, so it would have to wait.

Rubbing her back, it seemed like she was done so I asked her if she wanted anything. She shook her head no, so I guided her to the bed to lay her down. I was going to get her a warm ginger ale and some crackers even if she didn't want it right now though. When I got back up to the room she was still laying in the same spot, but there was a look of misery plastered on her face. Toya didn't get sick so her being sick like this could only mean one thing. And I was not ready for the answer, but I needed to ask.

"Latoya, are you pregnant?" I came straight out with it. There was no point in sugarcoating right now. She pointed over to the dresser and I peeped a small box that had a bow wrapped around it. I wanted an actual answer out of her, but I guess this would do. I didn't even have to open it to know that she was telling me yes.

Walking over to the bed, I sat beside her and reached over to put the box on the table. "So you're pregnant huh? How far?"

I didn't mean for it to come out like that, but I was shocked. We did have sex a few weeks ago when I was tore up, but aside from that, we haven't been doing anything. I barely even kissed her these days.

"Yeah, I am T.J. Is that a problem?" she snapped.

"Did I say that shit? I can't ask? Damn." I snapped back. "I just wanted to know how far along you were. Is that a problem for you?" I asked.

"It's yours!" she screamed. "Or do you not believe that?" she snapped at me.

"When's your first appointment?" I asked, avoiding her stupid ass question.

"I didn't make one yet. I need time to process." I nodded my head, forcing my arm around her.

"Thank you," I said kissing her forehead. "Thank you for making me a father; we're in this together," I said sincerely. I didn't know if I was ready for this but she was pregnant and I really didn't have a choice but to get there.

She didn't say anything else and I guess that was my cue to get up. I walked down to my man cave so I could have a drink and process my thoughts. I didn't know how I was going to tell my mom and I damn sure didn't know how I was going to tell Averi. She should have been the last person on my mind in a situation like this, but I couldn't help but feel obligated. I guess this is what they mean when they say don't leave the one you love, for the one you like...

ELEVEN

LATOYA

I was sick as shit and just wanted to lay in bed all day. I felt horrible and if this is what being pregnant is like, I'm not doing it a second time. I can't believe I got myself into this situation anyway. A few times. I miss a pill a few times and this shit happens. I'm actually surprised Tre didn't have anything to say about it, but I wouldn't worry about that. What I was really worried about, was whose baby it is.

Lately, me and Jayshawn have been fooling around like crazy. But there was one night Tre came in the house messed up and we ended up having sex. I had sex with

Jayshawn the night before and I was going on a few weeks pregnant. I didn't know how far along, but I would find out when I went to the doctor.

Deep down inside, my gut is telling me whose baby it is, but I don't want to believe it's Jayshawn's. Even though he does everything I wish Tre would do financially, it's Tre that I love, so I was going to have to cut Jay loose.

He was starting to get way too possessive these days. I mean I know Diva said he would, but I didn't think it would be this bad. Calling me at any hour, texting me nonstop, and buying me all types of things. I can't say I didn't like the gifts and money though. I just wish it was coming from Tre. Hopefully we can get back to a good place, so we can raise this baby together and I can secure a spot in his life forever.

And I didn't forget about Lacey's little nosey ass seeing me with Jay the other day at the plaza. I don't know what she was there for anyway, and I'm sure Averi's little bougie ass was with her too. That area wasn't somewhere they would be caught hanging around, so something was definitely up. As long as neither one of them opened their mouths about anything, my little secret could remain my little secret for a while longer.

I couldn't go back to sleep, so I decided to call Diva and see what she was up to.

"Hello?" she answered all groggily.

"Bitch, what you doin'?"

"Layin' down. I just woke back up a few minutes ago. You know my brother is lookin' for you, right?" she asked. And I rolled my eyes.

"I figured he was. I've been sleep," I lied. "That's why I haven't been returning any of his texts," I continued.

"Mmcht," she sucked her teeth. "Well he said he's been

telling you to come over. I'm sure you read that in the texts he sent."

"I did but I'm not feelin' that good today. I'm gonna let him know that it'll have to be another time."

"I don't think you heard me Latoya. He's *telling* you to come over here. And if he has to go out lookin' for you, it won't be good. That's why I told your little stupid ass to be careful. You thought I was playin' when I told you about him? Think about why he just got out Latoya," she finished, making my heart beat faster than it ever has. I was silent for a little while, until Diva said something else.

"I gotta go, but if I were you, I would just get over here." With that, she hung up and I was left with my thoughts. I know I needed to do something about her brother. I just didn't know what I could do right now. Especially now that I'm pregnant.

Gaining enough strength, I pulled myself out of the bed so I could go get it together. Grabbing my phone, it vibrated as soon as I picked it up; a text from Jayshawn. *Get over to my crib, now.* I didn't like the way I read that text and it had me even more scared. Taking heed to Diva's warning, I got a shower, brushed my teeth and left the house in a hurry.

When I got to their house, I shut the car off and went straight inside. And the first person I saw was Jay when I did. I rolled my eyes when he turned his back to me, but when he turned around to face me, I was all smiles.

"Wassup bae," he said, making me cringe a little. It wasn't a disturbed cringe; it was more out of fear. He said it with so much possession, it made me rethink everything I was doing.

"Hey," I said shyly.

"Why you actin' all funny?" He walked closer to give

me a hug and I hugged him back just to make things feel normal, even though I felt otherwise.

"I'm not. Where's Diva?" I asked. I didn't want to be alone with him right now. Even though I was feeling a little better, the nausea was still there and I knew I could get sick again at any moment.

"Upstairs sleep. You sure you aight?" he asked again. "I know what you need, hold up," he said, walking toward the kitchen. When he came back, he had a drink in his hand and I noticed a blunt rolled behind his ear. "Here," he tried handing me the glass, but I declined.

"No thanks, not today." He looked at me with a weird expression, and I knew it was about to be some shit behind it. I never rejected a drink and he knew that from the past few weeks I've been here.

"Aight," he said nonchalantly. I was honestly surprised he let the conversation go that easily, but that was short-lived when he asked me the question I was dreading coming out of his mouth. "Wassup with you? You pregnant or somethin'?"

Gulping hard, I said, "No, just not feeling good. That's why I wasn't returning your texts or calls. I was in bed resting." He didn't say anything after so I figured I was in the clear. But when he came over and sat down next to me, barely any space between us, I knew I wasn't.

He put his hand around my throat, not too hard but enough to apply some pressure. Putting his face close to mine and making sure his lips were close to my ear, he asked again. "Are you pregnant? And please don't lie to me," he said in that aggressive tone. And this time I couldn't. I just nodded my head.

Releasing the grip he had on my neck, he stood to his feet, pulling me up with him. Grabbing both sides of my face, he pulled me in for the sloppiest kiss I've ever received from him, and of course I reacted to it. Gripping me by the throat again, he whispered against my lips.

"She's respondin' to me ain't she?" he asked in a low, seductive tone.

"Mhm," was all I could get out. Reaching into the shorts I had on, he ran one of his fingers across my middle and my legs almost gave out. He repeated the motion a few times before I released against both of his fingers. He then kissed me again and I knew we would finish what he started, but he surprised me when he backed away from me, licking both of his fingers.

"You ain't gettin' none of this, not today lil mama. Don't lie to me again." Winking at me, he turned toward the stairs and as he was going up, Diva was coming down.

"Mmcht," she sucked her teeth again. "You done messed up. You need to figure something out Latoya, forreal," she warned, looking behind her. And I just waved her off, but the look on her face told me she was serious. I was never one to fear anything but right about now, I was scared as hell. I knew one thing. It was too damn late to turn back now.

It's been a busy few weeks and I just wanted a small break from reality for a little. Between my job, what I'm working on with Lacey, and Josiah wanting to plan this wedding so soon, I am drained. I was so glad I didn't have a class today. I was overdue for some personal time and I figured I could just spend it with my mom. I just wanted to spend some mother-daughter time together and catch up on everything that's been going on.

Stepping out of the shower, I dried off and got changed into some comfortable clothes. I picked up my phone to call my mom and the first time it rang straight through, but when I called back a second time, she picked up.

"Hey baby," she answered.

"Hey ma, what are you doing?"

"At the hospital, it's gonna be a long day for me. What's going on? You sound stressed." Just like Lacey, my mom could always sense something was wrong just by the tone in my voice.

"Just a lot going on. Figured I could come by and we could catch up on things but I guess you're gonna be at the hospital all day," I sighed.

"Aww baby, I'm sorry, you know I don't come in unless I really need to. Sunday? I'll cook, you and Josiah can come over." Sighing, I just let her know I would talk to her later and hung up the phone.

I really wanted to talk to my mom without Jo around. I loved him to death, but I just wanted some girl time. I was about to go and lay down, but then I remembered Tre's mom. Even though me and him weren't speaking right now, she was like a second mom to me and has always been there when I needed her. I would just go over there. Grabbing my keys off the table, I raced downstairs and got in my car.

"Hey baby," Ms. Leslie greeted when I walked in. "You alright?"

"Yeah. Just had a free day for once, Jo isn't home, and I wanted to get out for a little. Hopefully have some girl time," I vented. I seen the eye roll at the mention of Josiah's name, but I didn't mention it. I understood how she felt, but at the end of the day the current situation isn't my fault; it's Tre's.

"Well you know I'm always here. I was just about to cook, come help." I knew she had to really have some type of love for me because she didn't even let Tre anywhere near her kitchen. She always prepared everything and would watch us eat it.

About an hour later, we had plates made and wine poured. Walking over to the table, I was about to start venting about the real issue, but Tre walking in the house stopped me from speaking. I seen him look at the ring on my finger and as quickly as he looked, he turned away even faster.

"Wassup beautiful," he greeted his mom, walking over and kissing her on the cheek. "What you make?" he asked, sniffing all over her plate.

"Boy," she said, smacking him upside the head. "Food, Averi made it," she said, winking at me. I just took a sip of my wine and a bite of food. "I'll make your plate." Walking off to the kitchen, she left us sitting there. When she brought his plate back, we sat and ate in silence. He finished his in a matter of seconds it seemed like and before he was about to ask for a second one, his mom cut him off.

"This is foolishness. Both of y'all are grown as hell and actin' like damn children," she snapped. "A damn shame." Huffing, she sat down next to Tre. "I'll bring your greedy ass another plate, but y'all are gonna talk and today. I'm tired of him moping and I know you wanted to talk about his stubborn ass too," she said putting me on blast.

"Talk and I mean it dammit." With finality, she snatched his plate and went to go put more food on it. When she came back, she threw it down and went upstairs.

"Well I guess she told us," I laughed, breaking the awkward silence.

"Yeah she did," Tre replied. "But she is right though Ave," he continued. "We have been actin' like kids over nothin'."

"You've been acting like a kid," I corrected. Nodding his

head, he took a bite of food. Breaking the silence again, I spoke, teasing him. "I'm assuming you're done with the personal sessions."

"Yeah," he replied. "After the first one, I don't even need all that pressure," laughing, he continued. "You're doin' your thing though, I'm proud of you forreal." And he flashed that perfect smile of his.

"Thank you Tre, I'm proud of you too," I returned the smile.

"And I apologize about everything. I can't even lie. I'm a little hurt about this situation," he said, pointing down at my finger.

"Why?" I asked.

"Nothing, forget what I just said. I'm happy for you Ave."

"Thank you Tre, I really appreciate that." Looking at his face, I knew there was more on his mind that he wanted to say and my prediction was correct. But what came out of his mouth, I definitely was not expecting.

"Latoya is pregnant," is what came out and I was stuck. *Pregnant?* I replayed in my head. "And despite me not being happy with her, I know I can't leave her alone right now. She and the baby need me," he concluded.

My mouth was open for what seemed like forever and before I was able to say a word, Tre's mom came from around the corner, speaking the exact words I couldn't get out.

"I know I didn't just hear that Tremaine Lamont Jackson," she fussed. "How could you allow yourself to get that little hussy pregnant?!" she yelled. Rubbing her temples, she took a seat on the couch.

"Ma, I-I–" he stuttered, not able to find his words either.

"Just shut up. I don't even want to hear anything out of

you boy," she fussed again. I have never seen her this angry, but I can't say that she didn't have a reason. This was crazy.

The next thing I heard was Tre getting popped upside the head. His mom moved quick. I didn't even see her get up from her spot on the couch.

"Ouch ma, damn," he whined. Rubbing the back of his head, he stared at me from across the table, looking me directly in the eye. "Averi," he started. "Say something, please."

"Congratulations Tre," I said holding tears back. "It sounds like you two have a lot to talk about, I'm just gonna go."

Learning that Latoya is pregnant brought back some unpleasant memories and it sucked that it still triggered me. A tear fell and he moved from his seat attempting to wipe it, but I swatted at his hands. Getting up from the table, he tried to reach for my arm, but I moved before he could.

"Tell your mom it was nice seeing her again and thanks for dinner. Congratulations again Tre, I know you'll make a great father." Grabbing my bag, I threw it over my shoulder before walking out and shutting the door behind me.

As soon as I got to the car, I looked at myself in the mirror and realized I had no reason to be crying over this situation. Getting cheated on does leave a lot of bad memories, but it happened in high school and I needed to work on moving past that. Looking down at my finger, I smiled and knew that this meant I was starting a new chapter in my life. And what happened in the past, needed to stay there.

"No I don't want those colors Jo," I complained. Picking up the next book, we flipped through that one in a matter of seconds, still not being able to decide on colors for the wedding.

I knew planning a wedding wasn't going to be the easiest, but I damn sure didn't think it would be this hard. Everything I liked, Jo disagreed with and what he liked, I didn't. It probably wouldn't be this difficult if he wasn't in such a rush to get married, but the plan he had set made sense and I was kind of excited so I went with it. The more we disagreed on things though, the more annoyed I got and was ready to push the date back.

"Don't you think this is something the bride and the ladies in her wedding should figure out?" his mom asked. And I was glad she said something.

"This is our wedding ma. I feel like I need a say," he whined like a kid. Rolling my eyes, I picked up another book.

"That's it Josiah," she snapped. "Let Averi pick out what she wants and you two can settle on something; this is ridiculous. She's the damn bride," she fussed. And with that last word, she got up to refill her wine glass.

Leaving the two of us in the living room, no words were spoken. All you could hear were the sounds of the pages flipping and Jo smacking on the damn food his mom brought over.

"I'm sorry bae," he apologized. "I'm just happy to be gettin' married to you and I wanna be a part of it," he said, sounding kind of sad. "But if you want me to leave it alone, I'll let you, Lacey, and our moms figure all this shit out."

"I do want you a part of it, babe, but we're doing too much disagreeing and I don't want to have an argument about it. That's what usually follows," I vented.

"That's why I'm gonna take a step back. I trust you baby girl, so just choose what you want. As long as you're walkin' down the aisle to marry me, I'm coo'." Getting up, he grabbed my hand to kiss the back of it and then kissed my lips. "I'm gonna go handle some business. Be ready when I get back," he winked. I already knew what that meant so I smirked and watched him go out the door.

His mom walked back in the room a few minutes after he left out and sat down next to me, helping me finish picking out colors.

"Averi, I need to get something off of my chest," his mom confessed. I didn't like the feeling I got from her saying that, but I gave her a look that let her know to continue. "I feel like something isn't right."

"I'm confused," I said truthfully. "What do you feel isn't right?"

"This. I love my son and I love you for him, but I feel like the wedding is so sudden. I don't know. I'm not trying to worry you baby or cause any issues. I'm just not feeling right."

I took in the words she said. Even though I felt some type of way, I didn't let it show. I wonder where her thoughts came from all of a sudden, but I wasn't going to worry about it at the moment. I just brushed off what she said and put it to the back of my mind so we could finish planning more of the wedding.

After about an hour, we got a little more done and Jo's mom said she was going to leave since she was getting tired. Walking her out, I cleaned up the kitchen and then went to straighten up the living room. After that was finished, I went upstairs so I could take a much needed bath. Getting the water to the perfect temperature, I sat in the tub, put my head back and enjoyed my playlist. I couldn't even enjoy two songs, before my phone was ringing.

Picking it up, I answered without even seeing who was calling.

"Hello?"

"Damn bitch, who has your panties all twisted?" It was Lacey. Rolling my eyes, I put her on speaker and laid my phone back down.

"If you must know, I'm trying to enjoy a soak in the tub. Jo's mom was just over here trying to help with the wedding."

"And how did that go?" she asked.

"Didn't get much figured out. I honestly need you and my mom," I admitted. I knew this wasn't going to work if I only had Josiah and his mother's help.

"I already know," she sassed. "But that's not why I called." *I'm already knowing.* "Did you want to go out tonight? A bitch is bored and being single doesn't help that."

"What happened to the dude you've been talking to?" She was just bragging about a guy not even a week ago saying that they were going to make it official and now she's talking about being single.

"He was a waste of time. You wanna come or not?" she asked. "Actually never mind, I'll see you in an hour. Bye," she hung up, not giving me a chance to respond. Rolling my eyes, I finished washing so I could get ready to go out with Lacey's crazy ass.

WALKING IN THE CLUB, Lacey spotted two open seats at the bar and that's where we were headed. Ordering my drink first, she was about to order hers until a deep voice spoke from behind her.

"What can I get the pretty lady to drink?" he asked. Blushing, she turned toward me and sent a wink my way. I smirked back and tuned them out so she could do her thing. About ten minutes later, she turned around, showing all thirty-two.

"Assuming that went well," I said, laughing.

"Damn right it did," she replied, still keeping her same energy. "He wrote his number down and told me whenever I'm ready to get taken out on a date, to call him." Nodding my head in approval, I took a sip of my drink and danced to the music that was playing. Two drinks later, I was feeling a little buzzed.

"L-Let's go dance Lace," I suggested.

"No ma'am, you can sit your buzzed ass down right here," she laughed. "Forgot you barely drink liquor, ol' prissy ass," she continued laughing. I rolled my eyes and tuned her out again, letting the music take over. But when I heard Josiah's name, it alerted me.

"What?" I asked.

"Is that Josiah over there in the corner?" Looking to where she was pointing, it sure was. He did mention earlier that he was going to handle some business, but what business was he doing that it had to be handled in a nightclub?

"Yeah it is," I said to myself more than to Lacey. "I'm about to text him," I replied, pulling my phone out of my purse.

Hey, where are you? I sent. Both of us looking over at him, we watched as he checked his phone, but what got me is when he put it back in his pocket without texting back.

"Mmcht," Lace sucked her teeth. "If I were you, I would walk over there and see what's going on myself, since you're obviously not gonna get an answer out of him," she sassed. In any other moment I would have, but being that he just proposed, I didn't want to jump to conclusions.

"You know how I get Lacey," I pleaded. "What if it's nothing?" I asked.

"You won't know anything until you ask Averi, but to each his own. You ready?" she asked, obviously annoyed. She could have this attitude all she wanted to, but at the end of the day this is my relationship.

"Yeah," I said, matching the energy in her tone. We put our tips down and then walked toward the door. Taking one last look at the corner Jo was in, seeing him all wrapped up in his conversation without texting me back, hurt my feelings a little. But I kept it pushing out the door.

Pulling up to my house, me and Lacey spoke no words as I got out of the car. I understood that she had a problem with Jo, but she didn't have to take it out on me. She's allowed to have her own opinion about him, but I at least expected her to be happy because I'm happy. I guess I just think differently. She watched me unlock the door and as soon as I stepped foot in the house, she pressed the gas and sped off.

When I got out of the shower, I checked the clock on the nightstand and it was going on twelve. Checking my phone, I was about to send another text to Jo, but a text from him came in as soon as I was ready to press send. *Handling business baby, I told you. Omw now,* was his reply. Placing my phone on the stand, I got in bed and cut the lights off. I wasn't even going to wait up. I didn't know what kind of business Jo was out handling, but I didn't have a good feeling about any of it.

FOURTEEN
JOSIAH

I don't know what got into Averi, but she's been acting real different these days. The other day I told her I was out handling business and she texted me asking me where I was. She never did that and it had me looking at her funny. I wanted to ask her about it that night, but when I got to the crib, she was asleep. My baby looked so peaceful when she slept so I wasn't going to bother her that night. But ever since then, shit's been weird around the crib and I didn't like it. I would talk to her, though, but for now I had some more business to take care of.

Pulling up to the restaurant, I looked around to check my surroundings, then I made my way inside. Looking to my left, I saw just the person that was waiting on me and I walked over to the booth. Sliding in the seat, I ordered a drink and got straight to the point.

"I moved the wedding up to the date you gave me; she went for it," I started off saying.

"Good, just keep doing what you're doing so she can stay how she is. The more she's focused on you, the more she only worries about you and her job."

"Bet. How far along are you anyway?"

"A little over a month," Latoya replied. "I just left from a doctor's appointment," she said, sipping her drink. I nodded my head, knowing I would be getting married around the time she gives birth.

I knew Latoya from way back, so when she told me about seeing Averi over at Tre's mom's house, I took it upon myself to see what was going on. She thought I just wanted to drop her off at work one day, but I was really seeing if her ass was being sneaky. When I pulled up and seen her and dude chopping it up, I knew I had to lock her down sooner than expected. So I proposed. And Latoya popping up pregnant was just the icing on the cake. Keeping those two apart was a priority and it seemed to be working.

We finished our food and made plans to get together in another week or two, make sure everything was steady. Walking out, I checked my surroundings again before I made my way to my car. Pulling off from the restaurant, I made a stop to get some food so I could surprise Averi with her favorite. I was hoping it would soften up the tension that was going on around the house. I'd be damned if I told her how I was getting money.

My uncle's shop was cool, but I needed some extra shit.

So when one of my homeboys told me about this gambling shit he does, I was all in. As soon as he showed me the ropes, I was taking everybody's money. These boys bet on damn near everything and it was honestly like taking candy from a baby; that's how easy shit was. I was bringing in so much money, it was crazy. I knew Averi was going to get suspicious about it, but what she didn't know, wouldn't hurt her.

Turning on our street, I was surprised to see Averi's car still here, but I was thankful that it was. I knew we were gonna have to talk sooner or later, so I prepared myself for the conversation. Walking in the house, candles were lit, so I know she just finished cleaning. Setting the food down, I went to go find her. She was sitting in bed reading when I got to our room.

"I brought you some food baby," I started off saying. She nodded her head, never taking her eyes off the book. And that irritated me. "Averi, did you hear me?" I asked again.

"Yes Jo, I heard you. Thank you. I'll get it when I'm done with this chapter."

"Nah," I said, walking over to grab the book. "We're gonna talk 'cause I'm not about to deal with this attitude you got for however long you're tryna have it." I was over this shit. "What's wrong with you?"

"You. I tried talking to you the other day but you had to rush out and do business. Tried speaking to you about it before I left for work, but you didn't have time for any of it. Even tried texting you, but you ignored me. So excuse me if I don't want to talk right now."

I felt bad, but shit, I did have business to handle. I was out here trying not to lose our things in a bet, but she didn't need to know that. "I'm sorry baby, I've just been real busy."

"Yeah Jo, I know," she said sadly, getting up. Walking

toward her, I grabbed her up, making sure she couldn't go anywhere.

"Averi cut it out," I said sternly. "I'm sorry baby, okay? My uncle's just been workin' me like crazy and he let some people go, so I've been doin' a lot of other jobs besides my own. I'll talk to him about it, aight? I promise." I kissed her forehead.

"Alright Jo. I'll just go eat," she said, moving from out of my embrace. Rubbing my hands down my face, I let out a deep sigh and went to the bathroom to take a shower.

When I got out, I walked in and Averi was on the phone. The only thing I caught before she hung up was her saying she would be over soon.

"Where you goin'? I had plans for us tonight," I lied. I just didn't want her going anywhere, but I would make some if she stayed home.

"Lacey's. She needs my help with something. I'll be over there for a while, so don't look for me to come home anytime soon," she stated nonchalantly.

"What does she need help with?" I asked out of curiosity. Ever since she snuck and went to Tre's mom's house behind my back, I was a little suspicious when she said she was going anywhere other than work.

"A project." Throwing her stuff away, she grabbed her bag and got prepared to leave.

"What do you need a bag for if you're not staying over there?" She wasn't making my thoughts any better.

"I might stay. What's with all the questions?"

"You gettin' defensive?"

"Not at all. But you seem to have a million questions all of a sudden after I call you out on your shit. Look, I'm going. I'll call you later," she argued, brushing past me. Not even a minute later, I heard the front door shut.

I was about to go after her, but I would wait. I didn't feel like arguing and she had a point. Going over to the closet, I pulled my clothes back and went into the box where I kept my weed. Taking out a bag and a blunt, I rolled one to perfection and lit it. Putting my head back, I blew out the smoke and seen my phone light up with a message. *Come get some money.* That was all I needed to see before I put the blunt out and left out the house.

"This shit is crazy," Averi whined.

"Look, you want to see what's going on or not? I could be out with Malcolm, but I'm trying to help you out," I complained. I loved Averi, but this shit with Josiah was starting to get on my nerves. Why constantly complain about something if you're going to allow it to continue.

"No, never mind," she said. And I rolled my eyes. "Let's just go back to your house."

"If we go back to my house, I'm going out with Malcolm, so you'll be there by yourself," I said truthfully.

"Then I'll just go back home." Shrugging my shoulders, I turned the car around and went back in the direction of my house. When I parked, Averi went straight to her car and I went in the house. I didn't have time for that tonight; I would check on her tomorrow.

After I got out of the shower, I dried my hair and decided on an outfit. I was excited to go out. It's been a while since I've been on a real date and I was hoping Malcolm wasn't a bust like the last person I was bragging on. But only time would tell.

Getting dressed in a black bodycon dress with laced up heels, I applied a little bit of makeup, put on my accessories and waited for Malcolm to arrive. I was in the mirror perfecting my hair a little more when I heard the doorbell ring. Spraying my hair one last time, I sashayed to get the door. And when I opened it, Malcolm was standing on the other side looking so handsome, a dozen roses in his hand.

"For you beautiful," he greeted, handing me the flowers. I smelled them and smiled.

"Thank you," I blushed. "Come in." Stepping to the side, I went to the kitchen to put the roses in a glass and then I met Malcolm back in my living room.

"This is comfortable," he said. "You decorated this yourself?"

"Yeah, majority of it. My best friend helped for a little of it though."

"Word? I could use you when I move into my new spot in a couple months, well that's if you stick around," he winked.

"Play your cards right and you won't have to worry about me going anywhere," I sassed back. We shared a smile and he looked away, admiring my decorations, while I took in the sight of him.

He looked fine at the club, but seeing him sitting on the couch right now, fine was an understatement. This man was beautiful and I really hoped he ended up being a good one. His skin was mocha chocolate, he had a clean low cut. His muscles were definitely present in the button up he was dressed in and he smelled so good. That smile of his was so perfect and his lips looked so soft. I was so into undressing him with my eyes that I didn't even hear what he said to me.

"Did you hear me Lacey?" he asked, staring me in the eye.

"N-No, sorry," I laughed it off. "What did you say?"

"I asked if you were ready to head out of here."

"Yes, I am." He rose from the couch first and then extended his arm out. Walking toward the door, he opened it and said, "Ladies first." Smiling, I stepped outside with him following behind me. Turning to lock the door, we walked to his car and we made our way to the restaurant.

"TWO FOR HOLMES." The host looked up the reservation and then we were led to a booth shortly after.

Sitting down, on the outside I was calm, but on the inside I was beaming. This restaurant had the best steak and it's been well over a year since I've eaten here. And it was expensive. I didn't want Malcolm to feel like he had to cover the whole bill either, so I spoke up about it.

"We can go half on the bill Malcolm." He didn't say anything, so I repeated myself.

"I ignored you for a reason Lacey," he said, never taking his eyes off the menu. "When I ask you out, you don't need to worry about touching your wallet. You hear me?" This time he looked me straight in the eye.

"Yes," was all that came out. He nodded his head and

then we proceeded to order our food. When the waiter took the menus, Malcolm started the conversation off.

"So Ms. Lacey, what is your passion?"

"Well I've always been into fashion and design. I started doing nails a little while ago and I'm waiting to hear back about this place that's available, hopefully it's a potential nail salon for me. And my best friend is starting a fitness line, I'm helping her design those clothes."

"A woman with a plan, I like that. Did you go to school?"

"I did, I graduated with my Bachelor's in General Studies since I didn't know what I wanted to do just yet. So if this doesn't work out, I always have a degree to fall back on, you know?"

"I definitely do, that's smart as hell."

Smiling, I asked him a few questions. "How old are you? Any children?" I figured since we were past what we did for a living, it could get a little more personal.

Laughing, he answered my questions with ease. "I just turned twenty-six and no kids. You didn't ask, but I haven't been in a relationship for three years, goin' on four."

"If you don't mind me asking, why is that?" I sipped my wine.

"She didn't match the walk she talked. Saying one thing and doing the opposite. We would communicate, but she lacked comprehension. Just felt like I was talkin' to a brick wall the majority of the time. Over time I just got tired, so I ended it. Shit wasn't gonna be fair to me in the long run, feel me?" He asked and I did.

The conversation with him was flowing so well, there wasn't a time I had to think of what we could talk about. He wanted to order another round of drinks, so I let him and went off to the bathroom.

When I walked in, the devil herself was at the sink, looking at her ugly ass reflection. Ignoring her, I went into a stall to handle my business. I thought that would stop her from saying anything to me, but boy was I wrong.

"Tell your little friend to stay away from my man," she said from the other side of the door.

"Might be the other way around baby girl," I replied back smartly. "Check your man." With that, I unlocked the door and pushed it open, knowing she was standing right in front of it. I was sure the door hit some part of her face since she backed away holding her nose.

"Bitch! I'm pregnant!" she yelled.

"Your face isn't," I retorted. "Next time move." Walking to the sink, I washed my hands clean and dried them. Throwing the towels in the trash, I walked out leaving the other trash looking pathetic.

When I got back to the table, there was an unopened bottle of wine with a brand new glass.

"Why didn't you pour it?" I asked curiously.

"I'd rather you pour it yourself. With all the shit happening these days, women should do shit like this themselves anyway." *A man,* I thought. Smiling, I poured my glass and then we clinked.

PULLING his car up to my house, Malcolm put it in park and we sat for a few minutes in silence. It wasn't an awkward silence, just both of us in our thoughts. I wanted to know what he was thinking, but I wasn't going to ask. Instead I asked if he wanted to come in or end the night right here.

"That's up to you beautiful."

"I just don't want you to look at me any different if we take it a step further tonight, you know?"

"I'm not a kid, I'm a grown ass man. If we cross that line, that's okay. And if we don't, that's okay too. To me, it doesn't matter if you wait one night or sixty-three days, if a man isn't interested like that, he's gonna leave after he gets what he wants." He shrugged his shoulders and I agreed. I was going to add my two cents, but he continued speaking.

"It's early I know, but after tonight, I know that I'm interested in taking you on another date, and another one, and another one after that. Only if you would like that as well." Finishing his sentence, he leaned over to kiss me and I met him in the middle. Moving our heads side to side, I was getting more into it and invited my tongue into his mouth, which he gladly accepted.

He was ready to pull me over the console onto his lap, but his phone ringing interrupted our moment. Letting out a frustrated sigh, he reached into his pocket and pulled out his ringing phone, answering with a little aggression in his tone. I wasn't able to make out what was being said on the other line, but when he yelled frustratedly, I knew whatever it was couldn't be good.

"Is he aight?" he asked the person on the other end. Nodding his head, he hung up the phone and started the car. "You wanna ride or you stayin'?"

"What's happening?" I asked worriedly. The anger and frustration in his tone kind of scared me and I wasn't sure if I wanted to stay or leave him at this moment.

"My little brother just got robbed," he admitted. "I need to go see wassup with him, but I need to go now. Are you stay—" he started, but I cut him off.

"I'll go with you," I answered. And he sped off.

The ride was silent and I wasn't even sure if I should

say anything. I hoped his brother was okay but the way Malcolm looked, I knew if he found out who did it, that person would be in for a rude awakening. We ended up parking in front of a house that looked kind of rundown, but I wasn't going to say anything about it. I was here for support.

Malcolm got out and then he walked around to open my door. When we walked up the porch, he knocked and the door swung open not even a second later. Walking in, I moved a little slow just because I was unfamiliar with the place and he grabbed my hand and placed a kiss on the back of it, mouthing to me that everything was alright. I breathed a sigh of relief and he chuckled. I was just glad I could make him smile at this time.

He guided me over to the couch with him and sat me on his lap. A few minutes later, a bulky guy walked from the back and shook Malcolm's hand. He extended his hand to me and I looked down at it, then looked to Malcolm. Nodding his head letting me know it was okay, I shook his hand and he smirked at me.

"Got a nice one boy," he complimented.

"Don't I know it," he replied, giving my thigh a light tap. And I smiled to myself. This man was making me blush a little too much tonight, but I can't say that I didn't like it. "What happened Roc?" he asked the guy.

"You wanna talk about it in front of ya lady?" he said, making sure. I didn't take offense to it.

"It's straight. What happened?" And he got into it. I tried to tune them out as best as I could because it wasn't my business, but when one name was mentioned, I couldn't help but to listen.

"This Josiah cat, you know where he stays at?" Malcolm asked. And I got worried. Not for Josiah, but for Averi. I didn't need anything happening to my best friend over his no good ass.

"Nah, but he was seen at that popular car spot not too long ago. Looked like he was in uniform. Should we catch 'em there?"

"You good. Since it was my lil' bro, I'm gonna let him figure out how he wants to deal with it. You know he'll handle it. I done told him about this gambling shit," Malcolm stressed. *Gambling?*

"Bet. Your brother said he's cool though; they got his phone so he used one of the chicks he was with," the guy laughed. "He'll get up with everybody tomorrow." Nodding his head, Malcolm whispered to me, asking if I was ready to go. I nodded my head and after he said his goodbyes, we were on our way back to my house.

With his hand on my thigh, I stared at him throughout the entire ride. When we pulled in front of my house, I reached for my seatbelt, but Malcolm put his arm out.

"Sorry about tonight," he apologized. "I don't want you to think I'm into any type of shit, it's my little brother. I'm tryna get him on the right path. Shit ain't workin' though." I could tell he was frustrated, but you can only help someone who wants it.

"I hate to say this, but maybe something like this had to happen for him to get it. A hard head makes a soft ass you know." And he let out a light chuckle.

"You're definitely right about that," he said, still smirking. There was a little silence after that, until he looked my way and our eyes locked. He grabbed my chin, pulling me toward him and he brought my lips to his. After a few more pecks, we backed away.

"Go on and get in the house," he said. "I'll call you when I get home, aight beautiful?" I smiled, nodding my head. Leaning over the console, I gave him one last peck before I sashayed my way to the door. And as soon as I walked in, he drove off.

Putting my back against the door, I couldn't believe how perfect this night turned out to be. Aside from the situation with his brother, I didn't have any complaints and I couldn't wait until I seen him again. Taking off my shoes at the door, I threw them to the side. I would clean up tomorrow. What I didn't know was how or when I was going to tell Averi what I found out tonight...

Rolling over, I didn't know what time it was, but I was tired as hell. Snatching my phone off the table, I looked at the caller ID and it was Lacey calling. It was well after 1 A.M., so it must have been important.

"Hello?" I answered, worry in my voice.

"Averi, we need to talk," she started off saying. And she wasn't making my feeling any better.

"What is it Lacey? It's after one and I'm worried. What's wrong with you?"

"It's not me, it's Josiah. Look, I was out with Malcolm

tonight and when he was dropping me off home, he got a call about his brother. He was robbed." She took a short pause after that.

"Okay, Lace. What happened?" I did want to hear about her date but I knew right now wasn't the time.

"Sorry. He was robbed and Josiah's name came up!" She yelled. And hearing his name had me sitting up on the couch. "I tuned them out but when I heard his name, my ears perked up. He mentioned something about gambling too. They know where he works and everything Averi. I don't know if it was him that did it or not, but the fact that Josiah's name came up, didn't give me a good feeling."

She finished her peace and I sat in shock. I didn't want to believe any of what she was saying but all of his recent behavior showed signs. The extra money he was bringing in, the late nights he was having, all of it just made sense. And being that he wasn't home right now, didn't make his case any better.

"Averi!" Lacey yelled again. "You there?"

"Yeah Lace. Listen, thanks for telling me all of that, but I know what I need to do."

"Do you want to come over?"

"No, I'll be okay. I have to handle this. But I wanna know about that date," I said, getting a laugh out of her.

"Of course bitch," she laughed. "And I'm sorry about the other day, I love you and I just don't want to see you hurt."

"I love you too and no one wants to see their sister hurting," I said truthfully. "But you won't have to. Let's do lunch tomorrow?" I asked and she agreed. Hanging up with her a few minutes later, I went upstairs to get dressed in a sweatsuit, put on some Nike sneakers and I wrapped my hair up.

Putting some more clothes and products in my bag, I zipped it up and left out the room.

Coming back downstairs, I sat on the couch waiting for Jo to walk through the door. Taking a look at the clock, it was going on two and I wondered what he could say about coming in the house this late. I waited about another half an hour before I saw headlights pulling up in the driveway. Sliding the jacket to my sweatsuit off, I stuffed it in my bag and propped my feet up. The door opened and Jo waltzed in like it wasn't going on three in the morning.

"Nice of you to make it home Josiah," I said, scaring him. It was pitch black downstairs and I know he wasn't expecting me to be down here.

"What the fuck Averi," he almost screamed, his voice rising higher than it should have. *Punk ass.* "The fuck are you doin' sittin' in the dark like this?" Cutting the light on, he started toward me until he saw the look that was plastered across my face.

"The better question is, why are you coming in the house at this time? I know for a fact your uncle's shop doesn't stay open this damn late, so where have you been?" The frustration and irritation was present in my tone and this time nobody was going anywhere until some questions were answered.

"I was out handling business Averi, damn. All this insecure shit is gonna get old quick," he had the nerve to retort.

"Insecure?" I scoffed. "Far from it. Excuse me for wondering where the fuck my man has been all damn day, since he doesn't like to answer phone calls or texts anymore." And here I was, hot all over again. I swear only Josiah could bring this much anger out of me.

"I told you, but you questioning me isn't backin' up your statement Averi. Chill the fuck out."

"Talk about questions and insecurity," I laughed more to myself than out loud. "And exactly how many questions have you been asking me lately? Most of them about a whole other dude. Who's really insecure here?"

His nostrils flared and I knew that he was starting to get pissed, but I didn't care. He wanted to start, and I was damn sure going to finish it. Crossing my arms, I got a little more comfortable on the couch so the conversation could continue.

"Ain't shit about me insecure. I was makin' sure you weren't out bein' fuckin' sneaky," he tried to say. Scoffing again, I knew this wasn't going to last much longer. He was just digging himself in a deeper hole.

"You wanna talk about sneaky?" I tossed my head back a little so I could mentally prepare for the blow up that was about to happen. "Where is all of this extra money coming from Jo? And don't give me that bullshit about your uncle's car shop doing good." Tilting my head to the side, I waited for his reply. He turned his head, so I continued.

"And these late nights?" Still no answer. I was about to continue again, but he cut me off.

"Fuck! Averi, damn," he snapped. *And there it is.* "You wanna know the truth? My uncle's shop isn't puttin' shit in my pocket, so I started fuckin' gambling. That's where all of these late nights are comin' from."

"Gambling Josiah? Have you lost your fuckin' mind? Do you know what happens when you bet all heavy like that? Is that where that black car came from the day you picked me up from work?"

"Yeah it is Averi. And you wanna know somethin' else? I didn't get fired from that old job. I quit that bitch," he admitted. "You think you the shit 'cause you have your own business?" he asked. "That's the main reason I'm stickin' this shit out with you." And that was like a stab to the heart. "Wait bab–" he started, but I wasn't hearing anymore.

On the outside, I wasn't showing any emotion but on the inside, I was hurting. To hear the person that I've been with all of this time was only around because I had things going for myself, hurt. And I don't think there is any coming back from this.

Calmly sliding the ring off my finger, I tossed it at Josiah and watched it fall to the floor. Getting up from the couch, I grabbed my bag and my keys off the table and started to walk out of the door. Josiah tried to grab my arm, but I snatched it away and walked outside.

Speed walking to the car, I hurriedly unlocked the doors so I could get in. Tossing my bag in the backseat, I was about to back out of the driveway, but Josiah was standing right behind my car.

"Averi! Get out the car baby please," he begged. I pressed on the gas and he jumped out of the way before I hit him. Speeding off, I took off in the direction of the only person that could make me feel better right now. Knocking on the door, I waited for about a minute and as soon as the door swung open, I burst out in tears.

Latoya was going on five months pregnant and shit still wasn't getting better with us. I was enjoying going through this pregnancy with her and seeing my little man on the screen, but other than that, I was miserable. I took a break from going to the gym and just kept everything strictly about my business so I could focus on Toya and the baby, but it wasn't working out in my favor. She was starting to take advantage of it and I had to do something about it. And I missed seeing Averi.

It's been a little while since I saw her and even though I

know I was feeling her more than I let on, I did just miss being in her presence. Latoya was going over her friend's house today and that was perfect for me. I felt like I needed to slide up to the gym and see what Averi had going. After Toya was dressed, she took the food I made her and left. Waiting twenty minutes, I hopped in my truck and drove to the gym.

On the way, my hands were sweaty and my stomach was in knots. I really felt like shit that I put myself back in this position with Averi, after we were in a decent spot. After the last time I saw her at my mom's, I decided to call her and we had a long conversation. How we both moved on and our friendship was more important. But I couldn't keep lying about my feelings, her being engaged or not.

Parking my truck, I looked in the lot for her car, but I didn't see it. Walking into the gym, I signed in and when I looked to my left, I saw her in a classroom doing what she does best. I didn't know if the class just got started or not, but I was going to stick around until it was over. Going to the locker room, I changed into some workout clothes and occupied myself until she was finished.

A half an hour later, I saw everyone coming out of the classroom, sweat dripping and all. She really does her thing in there. Putting the weights back where they were, I grabbed my water bottle up and jogged over to the classroom. When she walked out, she looked a little shocked to see me, but she smiled and gave me a hug.

"Hey Tre, I haven't seen you by here in a while." Taking a sip from her water bottle, she took her towel and wiped the sweat from across her forehead.

"Yeah I know. I've been a little tied up with Latoya and the baby," I admitted, sadly.

"Is everything okay?" she asked concerned.

"Nah Averi, it's not. I should've been told you this but when we talked, it wasn't the right time." I took a pause so I could take in the perfect sight of her and when she lifted her arm to put the towel around her neck, I saw that her hand was ringless. "Come out with me."

She looked at me skeptically and I just gave her another one of my looks. Walking away, she went back in the classroom to get the room and her stuff together. Five minutes later, she walked back out asking where we were going.

"It's a surprise," I told her. Laughing, I knew she hated surprises, but this would be a good one.

PULLING up to the surprise place, I got out of the truck and ran around to open Averi's side. Making sure the blindfold I made was put securely over her eyes, I helped her out and guided her toward the door. When we made it in, I took the blindfold from around her eyes and she looked around trying to figure out where we were. But when she saw the sign over the bar area, she turned around to me with her mouth wide open.

"Tre!" she yelled, pushing my arm. "You opened your second bar!" I knew she was excited because she kept yelling.

Laughing, I nodded my head and started walking so she could get a tour of the place. "Yeah, the opening got pushed back, but she's finished. And you're the first to see," I truthfully admitted.

"Stop playing," she said, but I wasn't.

"Dead ass Ave." All seriousness in my tone. When the bar was finally finished, Averi was the first person I wanted to call and tell, but showing her was even better.

"I'm so proud of you Tre," she sincerely said, giving me

a hug. And I needed this. Even though she just got done working out, she still smelled good. She was perfect.

"Thank you," I whispered. We broke apart after what seemed like forever and there was a little silence, until she spoke.

"Show me around," she said. "And you better be feeding me," she laughed, but I knew she was serious.

"I got you fat ass," I laughed with her. Letting her walk in front of me, I showed her around my establishment.

Sitting down at one of the tables, I called one of my workers from the other bar to come down and cook a little something. He was one of my best and he was definitely going to get a raise soon. When he showed up, I broke him off with some extra cash for coming out and he went straight to the kitchen. A little while later, our wings and fries were placed on the table.

"So, how is everything?" I started off asking. I wanted to ask about the missing ring, but I would wait until she mentioned it, if she was going to.

"Good," she kept it short. I was a little disappointed, but then she started speaking again. "I just got my apparel in for the fitness line, so me and Lacey are getting that together. Still doing my classes and some personal sessions. Me and Josiah are done, that's really the only change." And there it is.

"What happened with you and ol' boy?" I questioned. I cared about everything else she just said, but I wanted to make sure I could speak my peace on this.

"He basically said he was only sticking our relationship out because I have things going for myself. I didn't tell him about the clothing line I had with Lacey but he probably found out about that too, with how sneaky he was starting to be. It's alright though, I've been dealing with it." I heard the sadness in her voice and I didn't want her sad over this nigga, but she was with him for a minute so I understood.

"That's fucked up Averi," I said, shaking my head. "You didn't need him, though. You're too good for him forreal." And I meant every word.

She was perfect, in every sense. And for him to say that shit, had me feeling some type of way. One of these days I would catch up with him but for now, I was focused on Averi. I would give her some time to get over her breakup though. Once she was, she was mine.

"Are you ready for fatherhood?" she asked, shutting my dreams down. Just that fast I forgot all about Latoya.

"Yeah," I said truthfully. "Seeing little man on the screen is dope, I'm not even gonna lie. I can't wait until he's actually here though."

"That's good, I'm so happy for you. What about you and Latoya?"

"That on the other hand, isn't workin' for me. I'm not tryna kick her out or anything while she's pregnant, but I can't do it anymore. My mind's not in it, my heart's not in it, I just can't. I'm not happy and it's not fair to either one of us."

She nodded her head, taking a few fries and stuffing them in her mouth. Looking at her, I wanted so badly to let her know how I felt about her, but I would just keep it to myself for now.

After she finished her food, I grabbed everything to throw it away. I thanked my worker again for coming out and gave him a little more cash. Leaving out, I locked up and then we made our way to my truck.

When we got back to the gym, I got out and then ran around to open Averi's door. As soon as she stepped out, there was a voice yelling her name.

"Averi!" She turned and I knew it was her ex because she started walking straight toward her car. He darted over there trying to catch up to her and that made me lock my doors so I could be right there close to her. "The fuck you doin' gettin' out of his car?" he asked aggressively.

She ignored him and kept walking. I wasn't too far behind, but he was getting closer to her, so I picked up my speed.

"Josiah, can you just go," she said. "I'm done alright and stop showing up to my job."

"Why were you gettin' out of his car Averi? I knew you was out bein' sneaky," he snapped. "Can't ever trust no damn body."

"My man chill out," I said to him. "She doesn't even want you here right now. And we go back a few, not that you need an explanation." He looked salty about that comment, but it wasn't my problem. "You need to go."

He looked to Averi again before he accepted his defeat and started walking the opposite way. Before he got too far, he turned around and gave Averi the most menacing stare and I didn't like the shit, at all.

"Yo Ave, you alright?" I asked. She didn't seem to be shaken up, but the way he looked, I wouldn't put anything past him right now.

"I'm fine Tre, thanks for that," she said sincerely.

"Has he been doing this since you called off the engagement?"

"He's just been blowing my phone up honestly. I moved out of the house since the lease was up soon anyway and I didn't tell him anything."

"Where have you been staying?"

"With Lacey," she admitted. And I felt good about that.

Lacey was as real as it got and I was glad Averi had somebody like her.

"My dawg," I said and we shared a laugh. "But I'll let you get goin'. I got something I need to do."

"Alright, I need to go make sure everything is ready to go with these designs anyway," she said and I nodded. Walking over to her, I gave her a hug and when we separated, it took me everything not to kiss her. Waiting until she got in her car, I watched her drive off and then I started walking toward my truck. *I needed to get this shit over with,* I thought.

Texting Latoya, I told her I needed to talk to her and it was important. She said that she was going to be at her girl's house for a little while longer and it frustrated me, but it wasn't such a bad thing because I needed a little more time to put everything together. Making a U-turn, I headed in the direction of my mom's house; I knew she would be able to help me out.

Using my key to unlock the door, I walked in and the smell of fried chicken invaded my nostrils. Making my way to the kitchen, my mom was pulling the baked mac and cheese out, along with a cake she made. Turning the pot off for the greens, I knew I would have to eat before I talked to her about anything.

"Hey beautiful," I greeted her, kissing her cheek. I knew better than to bother her when she was handling stuff over the stove.

"I just knew your fat ass was coming by; that's exactly why I made this," she replied back.

"Damn ma, your son can't even get no love?" I laughed. "That's cold."

"I carried your big ass around for nine months and then pushed you out. That's love right there." I couldn't even argue with that, so I went to go sit down at the table. After everything cooled off, she made me a plate. "What's going on Tremaine?" she asked.

"I come over here all the time ma," I said. "Why it gotta be somethin' wrong?"

"Because you're my son and I know when there's a problem with you. I could feel the energy when you first walked into my kitchen. You ain't foolin' no damn body," she retorted. "So what is it?"

After I took a few bites of food, I finally broke down and told her how I was feeling. I started with my current feelings toward Latoya and ended with how I feel about Averi. I even went as far as mentioning her ex and how I felt about what he was doing. When I was done, she looked at me with a look that told me she was about to give it to me straight.

"Now son, you know I love you to death," she started off saying. I didn't like where it was going, but I let her continue. "But you have to let it happen on its own time. I know how you feel about her, but I am also a woman at the end of the day. And you hurt her, bad." Putting my head in my hands, I felt defeated already.

"Pick your head up boy. I done taught you better than that." And that made me straighten up real quick. "I can still see the chemistry; it's there, but you can't force it. So don't tell her anything right now. She's fresh, she needs time, okay?" I nodded my head understanding where she was coming from. I hated when she was right, but I knew to listen to her right now.

"And what about Latoya?" I asked.

"What about her?" she snapped back. "If you're not happy, you leave, but don't neglect my unborn grandbaby in the process," she said sternly.

"Of course not ma, that's not even me. You and dad taught me better than that, God rest his soul."

My dad passed when I was a little boy. I was probably only four or five. I was told he got caught up with the wrong people and when he was out one night, he ended up being mistaken for another person. The guy who did it is in jail, but that shit won't bring my dad back. I only remember a few select memories, but I cherish those and the pictures we had almost every day.

My mom was silent for a few minutes, but she eventually got up and put my plate in the sink. Walking back to the table, she kissed my forehead.

"I love you," she said. "You're not happy, I can see it in your eyes. You already know what you have to do." And that was the last thing she said before she headed up the stairs. I did know and I know it needs to be done sooner than later.

Josiah

AVERI WAS STILL DUCKING and dodging me and I wasn't feeling that shit, at all. And when I showed up to her job to talk and she hopped out of that nigga's truck, I was heated. If she thought I believed that they were just friends after that, then she had me all the way messed up. We could discuss that when we got back together though. Right now I needed to work on getting her back.

The night she caught me coming in late and I said what I said to her, I felt like shit after. I was already pissed that night and her nagging just pushed me to saying all of that. Even though part of it was the truth, I was going to deny it like crazy. Aside from her having great money, Averi is as good as it gets and I'll be damned if I let anyone else have a chance with her.

I didn't know where she was staying at all and that was pissing me off too. I dropped by her parents' house a few times and even sat out there for hours, her car never showed up. I didn't know where Lacey lived but Latoya told me about the salon that she's about to open so I rode over there a few times. Averi was there once and I followed her after hoping she was going home, but she went to her job. I would get lucky one of these days, but for now, I was on my way to the gym to see if I could get her alone.

Parking, I got out of my car and looked myself over. I opened the backseat to get the gifts out that I needed and then shut the door. I knew she was off around this time so hopefully when she sees me and the gifts, it will put a smile on her face. I was walking toward the door, but didn't have to get far because she was coming out. And with that nigga right behind her.

"Here we go again," he said.

"Averi!" I yelled. "This is what you're doin'?"

She rubbed her temples, something she did when she got real irritated. But if anyone was going to be irritated, it was me. Here I am trying to do something nice to show her how sorry I am and she keeps having this nigga right by her side.

"Josiah not right now," she said, her lips pursed together tightly.

"Nah, now," I retorted. "You ain't pickin' up the phone, I don't know where you're stayin' and every time I come around here, this nigga is here. Wassup with that?"

"You're not that damn slow Jo. If I'm not answering your calls, I don't wanna talk. And I would appreciate if you stopped showing up to my job."

Scoffing, I said, "You showing out for him huh?" The look she gave me could kill but she took it there.

"Look, this shit ain't cool," he stepped in saying. "You might as well take them disappointing ass flowers back 'cause she doesn't look impressed," he finished.

"I didn't know your name was Averi my nigga," I said, taking a step toward him. "But since I'm talkin' to you, I'm tired of you poppin' up at my girl's job." I was pissed off now.

I knew Averi was getting fed up because her leg was shaking and she was tapping her foot. The look on her face didn't make it any better either. I thought she was ready to walk toward me but when she turned to go back inside, I lost it.

"Bitch, I know you heard me askin' you–" was all I could get out before I felt a punch to my right jaw. And it didn't stop there. The more I got hit, the more numb I got and I was ready to pass out until I heard the sound of Averi's voice yelling for him to stop.

"At my job?!" she yelled. "Both of you need to go and right now." This time she walked off past both of us and got into her car, not taking one look behind her. I know she saw how bad I looked on the ground and the fact that she didn't even want to help, was cold.

Taking one last look at me, Tre got in his truck and he sped off not much longer after Averi. Feeling the side of my face, it was throbbing and I knew it was swollen. I didn't even want to see what it looked like, but I would have to face it sooner or later.

Sliding into the front seat, I looked in the rearview mirror to take in the damage that was done to my face. My eye was starting to blacken and it was swollen, my lip was busted and still bleeding, and my jaw was starting to bruise.

This nigga handed it to me I'm not even gonna lie, but I had something for that in due time. Right now, I needed to get my shit together.

Calling Latoya, I told her she needed to meet me at my homeboy's spot. He lived out the way, so it was perfect. I needed to fill her in on everything and let her know that she needed to get control over this situation, fast. This was my second time seeing Tre near my girl and I was starting to think she wasn't doing what she needed to do.

"The fuck happened to you?" Shad asked when I walked in.

"Nothin'," I answered, irritated. I was still mad Tre got me like that, but Latoya would fix this shit.

"Yeah aight," he mumbled, walking to the back. Not even saying anything, I sat back and waited until Latoya got there.

About a half an hour went by before she was calling and letting me know she was there. I walked outside and told her to pull her car to the front and then I took her keys, telling her to go in the house. Even though Shad's house wasn't near my usual spots, I still needed to take precautions. Parking her car in his garage around back, I locked it up and then brought the keys back to her.

"What the hell happened to your face?" she asked, holding her stomach. She was due in a few months and she already looked like she was ready to deliver.

"Your nigga is what happened," I admitted. "All over Averi," I added, to see what her reaction would have been. Not like I was lying.

"Over Averi? What do you mean over Averi?!" She snapped.

"Exactly what I said. I say something to her and he rushes over and starts raining blows, I didn't even have time to react," I partially lied. "You need to get a handle on this situation," I demanded. I was tired of this shit. The more he was around Averi, the harder our plan to keep them apart was going to be.

"What do you think I'm doing," she snapped. "I don't know what's been up with him but I'm trying." I heard her voice crack and knew she was about to start crying.

Ever since Toya got pregnant, she turned soft. I know pregnancies mess with women's hormones and all, but this baby had her crying every time I turned around. And this situation with Averi and Tre wasn't making her emotions any better.

"Clearly it ain't workin'," I snapped back. "Now clean me up," I demanded. She looked at me funny, but then she did what I said. Part of the reason I was in this situation was because of her, so she needed to help in some way.

Waddling to the back, she went to go look for Shad. Taking a seat on the couch, I sat and waited for her to get back. When she did, she had alcohol, wipes and some bandages. Finally taking a seat next to me, she started nursing my face. I was pissed that it came to this, but I would stop at nothing to get my baby back. And Latoya better step her game up, or I would have to take care of this shit myself.

After I left Josiah's friend's house, I went straight home. It couldn't have been safe going the speed I was going while being pregnant, but I didn't care about any of that. My only concern was finding out why Tremaine was spending so much time with Averi and if that's why he was staying away from home so much.

Pulling into the driveway of our house, I was glad to see that his truck was parked. Rushing out of the car, I made sure I got in there before he tried to leave out again. When I found him, he was in the kitchen making something to eat, one of his knuckles wrapped in a bandage. I already knew what it was from, but hopefully I could get the truth out of him myself.

"What happened to you?" I asked.

"Nothin', I'm good," he answered dryly. Just from that answer, I knew this conversation wasn't going to go well, but it needed to be had.

"So what did you do today?" I set my things down on the island and made my way over by the stove.

"Checked on my bar, went to the gym to workout, now I'm here. Why wassup?" he asked all nonchalantly. And these bland ass answers were getting old quick.

"I can't ask?" I snapped. "I wanted to go get some things for our son earlier but you were missing in action," I lied. I was with Jay earlier and he got some things for the baby.

"You just did and I told you. You didn't call me either, so how was I supposed to know that? You know we could've went." He was right about that, but that doesn't matter right now. What matters is him sneaking around town with Averi when he has a whole pregnant girlfriend at home who needs his attention.

"Fuck that Tremaine," I said getting to the point. "What were you doing with Averi earlier?" I asked. "And why are you out here fighting over her?!" I didn't want to yell because I didn't want my son feeling my frustrations, but I was getting madder with every question I asked.

"You stalking me now Toya? What's wrong with you lately?"

"You're what's wrong!" I yelled, not being able to hold my tears back. "Averi's at your mom's house, you're spending your days with her and you're out here fighting over her?!" Crossing my arms, I let the tears roll down my face. I didn't care to wipe them right now.

"You wanna know why Toya?" He started. "I love her, I'm in love with her," he stated, breaking my heart into a million pieces. "I've been loved her and I probably always will. I'm not happy," he admitted. "And I can't keep lying to myself or to you; it's not fair to either one of us." He cut the stove off so he could give me his full and undivided attention.

"So that's it huh? Just fuck me and the baby? You're not even trying!" I yelled.

"I've been trying, but you ain't ever gonna change. All you care about is materialistic shit and what I can do for you; that's why you cheated on me in the first place, right?" he asked, breaking my heart even more. "I can't do it anymore."

Sniffling, I picked up the first thing I saw which was a spoon. His back was turned as he fixed his food so he didn't see it coming. It hit him in the middle of his back and when he turned around, I was scared as hell.

"What I tell you about that?" He asked. "Stop doin' shit you don't want done to you Toya, forreal." He walked over to the drawer to get something to eat with and then he finished. "And don't ever disrespect me like that. I'm gonna be there for my son regardless; he don't have nothin' to do with how I feel about you right now." And with that, he walked off to his man cave with his food, leaving me crying in the kitchen.

Sliding down the wall, I cried silently and put my knees as far as they could go. I knew something was wrong with Tre, but I didn't know he felt like this. I knew we were arguing a lot more than usual, but I didn't expect him to say that he was in love with Averi, it was a stab to my heart and I didn't know how the hell we were supposed to come back from this. Finally gathering enough strength, I forced myself to go lay on the couch and I eventually cried myself to sleep.

When I woke up, I looked at the time on the cable box and saw that it was after ten. Pulling myself up, I rubbed my belly and I felt my son kick.

"I know baby, I'm hungry too," I said to him. Making my way to the kitchen, I searched for a menu so I could order a pizza before the place closed. After I ordered, Tre came from out of his man cave, with the same look plastered on his face.

I watched him as he walked over to the fridge to take out a Gatorade. Twisting the cap off, he gulped it down in a matter of seconds and shot it into the recycling. I was sure he could feel my eyes on him, but he didn't turn my way. He was ready to walk back to where he came from, but the sound of me clearing my throat stopped him in his tracks.

"Where does this leave us Tremaine?" I asked. "I don't want to lose you, I'll do anything," I damn near begged. I was trying my hardest to keep my end of the plan me and Jo had set. If I wasn't pregnant, I probably would have gotten down on my knees.

"It leaves us as parents," he responded. "I tried and tried but I can't do it. And before you think this is all about Averi, it's not. She's just the icing on the cake." With every word he spoke, he was breaking my heart more and more.

"I know what I did in the past, but I thought we got past that. Tell me what I can do, please." The look on his face didn't change and right then, I knew my begging and pleading wasn't doing a damn thing. "So you're just going to leave me alone and pregnant?" I asked. *This was it.*

"There you go again," he scoffed. "Making this about you," he continued. "I'm not gonna leave you alone while you're carrying my child, I'm here for you," he said, sternly.

"But there's nothin' else you can do Toya. You already did it," he added.

"I'm gonna pay the rent for the year, so you can stay here if you want to. I'll be at my mom's until I move into my new spot in a few days." Hearing those words, hurt my heart and I don't even think he realizes how bad. All I could do was nod my head to what he said.

The doorbell rang, but instead of me going to get it, Tre offered and told me to sit down, that he would take care of it. It's the least he could do anyway. While he was at the door, I pulled my phone out and sent a text to Jay. I would take a minute to get over this while spending time with my other baby daddy, but this wasn't over between me and Tremaine by a longshot.

It had been a few days and Averi still wasn't talking to me. When I was at the gym she avoided all eye contact with me; she wouldn't answer my texts or calls and I was out of options. I can understand why she wasn't speaking to me, but I wasn't about to sit there and let her punk ass ex disrespect her. That shit was foul and I wasn't going to let it slide.

Averi could keep trying to ignore me if she wants to, but shit, she would thank me in the long run. And I missed her. She is all I thought about these days and since I had that conversation with Toya, it got worse. I needed to tell her how I felt and soon. Even if she didn't feel the same, I wanted to get this off my chest so at least she knew.

After I checked in on my first bar, I drove to the second to make sure everything was cool for the grand opening. The dates kept getting pushed back because of all the chaos in my personal life but I couldn't keep letting this shit affect my business. In a few days my second bar would be open and I didn't know how to feel, mostly excited but a little nervous. I would like for Averi to be by my side for the big day, even if it's as just a friend. Her being there would make everything complete, which is why I was on my way to the gym now.

I was getting a little hip to her routine, so I knew that she would be done with her class by the time I got there. And I was right. When I parked my truck, I saw people walking out, looking like they just got done with an intense workout. Hopping out, I jogged to the door and held it open for the rest of the people coming out and then I went to go catch Averi before she rushed out of here like she usually does.

"Ave!" I yelled. She turned around but as quickly as she turned toward me, she turned away, continuing to pack up her things. "Look I'm sorry about the other day," I apologized. "But please, can you please talk to me."

I didn't do the begging and pleading for anyone, not even my own mom sometimes, but Averi had a way of bringing out that side of me. Walking over to where she was, I cornered her, so she didn't have a choice but to listen to what I had to say. I was a big dude and compared to her size, she didn't stand a chance.

"What is it Tremaine?" She answered sassily. I know

she was mad and all, but I couldn't help but smile at her little attitude. She was so damn cute.

"I'm sorry," I admitted again. "It was wrong to pull that shit at your job, but I wasn't gonna let him disrespect you like that over some stupid shit like not takin' his punk ass back." I knew Averi long enough to knowthat the look on her face wasn't of anger; she softened it up and started speaking.

"I know you came from a good place and I'm not mad at you for beating his ass," she laughed. "But in front of my job, it's not a good look and I'm not trying to lose my position here over some shit like that. Especially not before I can open my own place." And I definitely understood where she was coming from.

"I know and again, I'm sorry for that. It wasn't cool and it'll never happen again," I said promisingly.

"Thank you," she replied sincerely. Gathering the rest of her things, she was about to sling her bag over her shoulder, but I grabbed it from her.

"I know you're probably sore and all that," I joked. I thought she was about to laugh, but she surprised me by agreeing. "Worked yourself to death these past days few huh?" I asked.

"Honestly yes," she laughed. "I started a new routine for my usual clients and it's taking a little while to get used to, but I'm good."

Looking her over before we started walking out, I was stuck on how beautiful this girl was. Everybody had their flaws but it was hard as hell to find one about Averi. She was damn near perfect and it wasn't all physical. Her soul was beautiful, her mind was amazing and she was so down to earth. I don't know how I allowed myself to fuck this one up messing around with Latoya, but I know I was about to right my wrong.

"Let's go to dinner," I blurted out. I know I should have asked, but I was eager to get her out so I could express my true feelings about her.

"Tremaine–" she started, but I cut her off before she could object.

"I'm not takin' no for an answer Ave," I admitted. "Let me take you out to dinner tonight, no strings." I added that to get her to agree, but I didn't believe that myself. I knew I was going to express my feelings to her sooner or later.

The stare she was giving me was intense and, at this point, I was kind of regretting asking her out. I felt as though I was waiting forever for an answer and when I was about to say she didn't have to, she gave me one.

"Okay," she said, making my heart speed up. "What time?" I let her know everything and we agreed that I would pick her up around seven. After I shut the door to her car and watched her drive off, I got in my truck and headed to my spot so I could get ready.

"YOU LOOK BEAUTIFUL," I complimented Averi when she opened the door.

She was wearing a nice, long black dress that had a slit on the side and stopped just before her ankles and the heels she wore were sexy as hell. The dress wasn't too tight; it fit her curves just right and the accessories she had on just added to her outfit. Her hair was curled to perfection and her face was all natural just how I liked it, her lips covered in gloss.

"Thank you," she smiled, showing off her beautiful smile.

I was about to say something else, but Lacey coming down the stairs in her usual overprotective best friend fashion stopped me.

"Take care of my sister," she threatened.

"I wouldn't do anything else." And I meant that. I know what I did back in high school, but that was a mistake I would never make again if I get the chance.

"Mhm," she scoffed. "Call me later," Lacey said to Averi. She nodded her head and then left us to it. Extending my arm out, she grabbed onto it and then I walked us to my truck. Opening her door, I watched as she got in and then I went over to my side.

Pulling up to the restaurant, I looked to the side of me and Averi's eyes got wide, as I expected.

"You did not," she said.

"I did." This was our favorite restaurant to come to when we were together. Every Friday I would take her out and we would come here most of the time. Giving my keys to the valet, I stepped out and walked around to let Averi out.

Letting her lead the way, I grabbed the door to open it and let her in. I haven't been here since we broke up, but the place still looked the same and brought back a lot of memories. After I checked us in, we were lead to our seats, and the waiter told us he would be right back to take our orders.

While we were looking over the menus, I took a glance at Averi while she studied hers. I don't know why she was doing that either since she got the same thing every time. A glazed salmon dinner with the glaze on the side, a side of French fries and seasoned rice. Usually she would get a soda to drink but since we are of age now, I'm assuming she would get a glass of wine or something like that.

When the waiter came back, he took both our drink orders and food orders since we both knew what we wanted. And just like I thought, she ordered her usual. He took our menus and said he would be right back with the drinks. Nodding my head, I let him go about his business.

"So dinner at our favorite, huh?" She asked, starting the conversation off. I don't know why I was so nervous right now, but being here with her in this moment really brought me back.

"Yeah, had to do somethin' nice, you know," I replied, hoping to turn the conversation in the direction I needed it to go in.

"For what?" *Here we go.* I was about to answer her, but the waiter came by with the drinks and I knew I needed to take a sip or few before I continued.

Looking into Averi's eyes, she was determined to get an answer and I think I was ready to give her one.

"Averi," I started. "I love you." The words came out so quick and that was all that came out. I didn't even have time to process. All I could do was sit and hope that she felt the same or we could at least work on it.

"This is what you asked me out for?" She asked. And that wasn't the answer I was hoping to get.

"Not entirely." Which necessarily wasn't a lie. I did bring her out to confess my true feelings to her, but I did want to spend a little alone time with her since she wasn't talking to me and I wanted to apologize for the shit I pulled at her job.

"Tre we can't do this," she said.

"Do what Averi?" I asked, my left eyebrow arched.

I couldn't read her expression, but it wasn't a bad one so I guess that was a good sign. Before she was able to say anything else, the waiter came back, carrying our hot plates on a tray. Setting her plate of food down first, he put down extra napkins and silverware, before doing the same to me.

"Anything else I can do for the lovely couple?" He asked. I looked to Averi and she looked back to me with the same expression on her face.

"No everything is perfect," Averi answered, shocking me. "Thank you." She flashed that beautiful smile of hers and then he left us to it.

Taking a bite of her food, she did the little happy dance most females did when they started eating. After a few bites of food and a couple sips of her wine, she wasted no time getting back to the conversation.

"We can't do this Tre, us," she said. "I just got out of my relationship with Jo a little bit ago and Latoya is pregnant. I don't know your situation, but I won't look like a fool again, for anyone," she stated.

"So you feel the same?" I asked. I would get back to everything she said, but right now I needed to know the answer to this.

"I never stopped," she admitted. And my heart was ready to beat out of my chest. "But I'm not ready for anything right now."

"Averi," I started. "I regret everything I put you through before and I swear on everything I would never do anything to hurt you again. Seeing you made me realize that I never stopped loving you and I would do just about anything to get that back." She was ready to interrupt, but I stopped her and finished speaking.

"And as for Latoya, that's done. I promise to you it is. We're just parents, nothing more and nothing less. I even moved into my new spot a couple days ago."

"I appreciate that Tre, but I don't know. It's just a lot to think about and I'm not ready."

I understood where she was coming from, and I damn sure wasn't trying to push her away by rushing her. I would have to take what she gave me and go with it. She didn't reject me, so that was a good start. But I couldn't help by asking where we stood at this moment.

"We're friends," she said shooting me down. "I just need time to think about everything." Nodding my head, I finished the rest of my shrimp and steak, putting our plates to the side.

The waiter came back with the check and after paying, I got Averi out of her seat and we walked to my truck. Walking outside, I could've sworn I saw Latoya's car driving off, but I didn't want to think too much of it. Opening the passenger door, I let Averi in and then I walked around to my side. Cutting the music up at a decent volume, I drove off in the direction of Lacey's house.

Parking in the front, I shut the car off so I could walk her to the door. Letting her out, I held her hand as she stepped down and we didn't let go until we were at the door. Standing a few feet behind her while she unlocked it, she turned to me and gave me a hug.

"Thank you for tonight Tre," she said as she hugged me. I pulled her in tighter, getting a whiff of the sweet smelling perfume she had on.

Pulling apart, I couldn't help but take a glance at her nice plump lips. Bringing my eyes up, we both looked at each other and I took a risk and leaned in to kiss her. Surprisingly she let me and I brought my hands to her face. And if the night wasn't a good one already, ending it with a genuine kiss from Averi sure did it.

Picking up the last box, me and Lacey put it on the moving truck and then got in my car to drive to my new apartment.

"You sure you want to move out all sudden?" Lacey asked. "You know damn well you can stay with me as long as you need to."

"I'm already knowing and I appreciate that, but I can't go one more weekend listening to you and Malcolm almost tear down the walls," I said half joking.

I loved that Lacey found someone and from what I've

seen, he looked to be a good guy. But what I'm not going to do is listen to her getting some every weekend. I loved her to death, but some things I just wasn't going to stick around for. So I started looking for my own place, it honestly was about that time anyway. I didn't want to feel like a bother and the only place I would allow myself to be at for a while is my parents' house.

Getting to my apartment, I unlocked the door and looked at the mess I would have to pack up soon. It wasn't getting done today though. The apartment was only a one bedroom, but it was nice and spacious, enough for me. I ordered all new furniture and only took the important things I would need from the old place I shared with Josiah.

Speaking of Jo, I hadn't heard anything from him these past couple months. I can't say that I wasn't happy about that though. I still can't believe the things he said to me the night we broke up, and the real reason he was with me. It amazes me how you never really know someone's true intentions. But it is what it is. He was out of my life and I've moved on from all of that.

Pulling out my phone, I texted Tre to see if he wanted to come over and help me get my apartment together. We've been spending a little more time together, and I was enjoying that. I still wasn't ready for anything and even though I was starting to feel him a little more than I cared to admit, I wouldn't tell him that right now. We were fine with what we were doing and that's how it needed to stay for the time being.

He told me he would be over in a little, so I started unpacking everything in the kitchen so I could have something cooked for when he got here. I asked Lacey if she was staying and she said she was having Malcolm come pick her up so I guess it would just be me and Tre. Going into the kitchen, I started to take the things I would need to make some shrimp scampi and I had a brand new bottle of wine I was waiting to open.

A few hours later after I cleaned up a little and got my bedroom together, I started on dinner. Tre texted and said he was about twenty minutes away, so I put the finishing touches on everything and had plates out so we could make them as soon as he made himself comfortable. Leaving the stove on warm, I ran upstairs to change into something comfortable, tied my hair up and came back downstairs just in time to hear the doorbell.

"It smells good in here," he said when he walked in. While he was smelling the house, I was smelling him as he walked past me to get to the living room. He always smelled so good. "For you," he handed me a card, flowers and a gift that was wrapped.

"Thank you," I said, setting everything down on the table. Leading the way to the kitchen, I fixed him a plate and poured a glass of wine. After doing the same for myself, I led the way back to the living room so we could watch a movie.

"Nah," he said laughing. "You bringin' back memories forreal." And I was. 'Love and Basketball' was our movie; there was never a time we weren't watching it when we were together all the time. Taking a sip of my wine and a bite of food, I sat back and enjoyed the dinner and movie.

I DON'T EVEN REMEMBER FALLING asleep, but when I woke up it was going on eleven. Looking next to me, Tre was still knocked out, his mouth hanging wide open. I was glad he didn't snore. Easing from up under him, I went to the kitchen to pour a glass of wine. Turning around, I ran right into Tre's muscular chest, almost letting out a scream.

Hitting him after I caught my breath, I said, "You scared me." And of course he laughed.

"My bad Ave," he said, still laughing. "You woke me up when you moved. I was comfortable as hell."

"Sorry," I said joining in on the laughter. He walked over to pour himself another drink and then we walked back to the living room. "You can stay here tonight if you want," I offered. He had a little to drink and even though I knew he could hold his, I didn't want him drinking and driving.

"If it's cool with you, I'll sleep down here." I nodded my head and finished my glass of wine so I could head upstairs and get him a blanket. I was about to go back downstairs but Tre scaring me again stopped me from doing so.

"You have one more time to do that shit," I said, smacking him in the arm.

Laughing, he snatched the blanket from me and held it under his arm. "My bad damn," he got out, still laughing. "I don't want to be by myself though," he said, poking out his bottom lip.

"Scary ass," I joked. "We can sleep downstairs since my bed isn't all the way together yet." Nodding his head, he led the way back down the stairs.

Laying the heavier blanket across the couch, I grabbed two pillows and laid them on one side. Finding a comfortable spot, Tre sat next to me, spreading the blanket I gave him over us and we watched movies until we found ourselves going to sleep again.

. . .

WAKING UP, I looked up and Tre wasn't there. Taking a peek at the clock, it was going on nine. Walking toward the kitchen, I didn't have to wonder where Tre was for much longer. He was standing over the stove finishing up breakfast.

"Good morning Ave," he greeted, passing me a glass of apple juice.

"Good morning," I replied, stealing a waffle.

"Still up to that same nasty ass shit huh?" He asked, laughing at me. Rolling my eyes, I bit into it, jokingly rolling my eyes to the back of my head.

"Ain't a thing change." When he finished the eggs, he put them on a plate and had everything set out on the counter. He made both of our plates and then we walked back to the living room to eat.

"So what are your plans for the day?" I asked after taking a bite of my food.

"Check on my spot. Opening is in a couple days and you better be there," he said seriously.

"Duh," I replied smartly. "I wouldn't miss it." I took a few more bites of food and then decided to ask a question I'm sure he would be shocked at. "How's Latoya and the baby?"

"Straight," he said keeping it short. "I check on him a few times a day to see if he's okay and if she needs anything; that's as far as it goes." Nodding my head, I finished the last of my plate before taking both of them to the kitchen sink.

"I'm gonna head out though," he said, putting his shoes on. "I'll get with you later, aight?" It was more of a statement than a question but I nodded my head and walked him out. Watching him get in his truck, he drove off and I locked up.

I was sure I killed the mood by asking about Latoya, but

I genuinely wanted to know. I know we confessed our feelings a couple of months ago and shared a kiss at the end of the night, which I was sure complicated things a little. And even though I was starting to have those giddy feelings for Tre all over again, I feel like we needed this friendship to see if things needed to go further. But only time will tell.

I was nearing the end of my pregnancy and I just wanted all of this to be over with. I didn't have Tre right now and even though Jay gave me and the baby anything we wanted, I didn't want to be with him. It was also getting hard trying to split the time between the two of them. I even had to convince them that my family just wanted to have a babyshower that was small and intimate. I couldn't risk anything coming out before I gave birth to this baby.

And Tre leaving me alone in this house alone made me sick to my stomach every day. I was spending time with Jay, but it wasn't what I wanted. I even went without eating sometimes and making myself sick, just so Tre could come by and check on me. But when he forced me to go to the hospital and he caught on to my antics, he limited how much he came by, but he would call and check on the baby every day. What I did was stupid, but I was desperate as hell.

It pissed me off that he wouldn't talk to me unless it had to do with the baby, but I would change that. I've been hearing about his grand opening to the second bar he's about to open and I was damn sure making an appearance. I let him get this little break, but it was time he got it together. He wasn't going to get rid of me that easy. As long as the plan for me giving birth went smoothly, Tre would be right back with me.

I was on my way to Diva's house now so I could spend a little time with Jay before I got ready to go to Tre's opening. Jay's possessive acts were so irritating and I wished damn near every day that I didn't take it there with him. I also wished I took Diva's warning serious that night. But it was too late to turn back now. I just had to get ready.

Pulling up to Diva's house, I took one look before I got out. I didn't want to be here but I decided to show for a little before Jay blew my phone up. Walking to the door, I was met by Jay before I even had a chance to knock. This is the irritating shit I can't stand.

"Wassup boo," he greeted. I don't know why but all of a sudden his greetings were so cringy. But I returned the energy and gave him a quick peck.

"Nothing, what did you want me over for?" My attitude was present and I was hoping he caught the fact that I didn't want to be here right now.

"What's wrong with you?" He asked, but I ignored his question and took a seat on the couch.

"I don't feel good Jay. I was in bed and you wanted me to come over here. I came before you started trippin'." After I said that, my son started moving around like crazy and I knew he felt the negative energy.

"Go upstairs and lay down then." And my attitude got even worse.

"I don't want to be over here right now Jay, damn!" I yelled. With every second I was here, I was getting even more pissed and my head was starting to pound. My son was moving like crazy and I just wanted to leave at this point.

"You lost ya mind yellin' like that. But you know what, take ya stupid ass on then," he said, dismissing me. When I finally got up, I stormed out, ready to get tonight over with.

PARKING down the street from the bar, I watched so I could figure out the perfect time to show my face. The outside was packed with people and I actually felt a little bad for the scene I was about to make. This baby had me turning a little soft but I brushed those feelings to the side so I could focus on what I needed to do.

A little more time went by and I finally seen Tre's truck pull up, the valet taking his keys and he stepped out. When he got out, he looked himself over and he looked so damn good, I couldn't help but react to his appearance. The thing that got me was when he walked around and opened the passenger side door, letting Averi out of the car. He then opened the backdoor, letting his mom out. I was ready to act a fool now but I had time.

Waiting for another twenty minutes, everyone started to

go inside and that's when I decided to finally get out of the car. Locking up, I waddled my ass toward the doors. When I got there, he had security posted, but me letting them know that I was carrying Tre's child, granted me the access I needed. Walking in, I was just in time for everyone putting their glass in the air and taking a sip of champagne.

When I spotted Tre, he really had the audacity to have Averi right by his side like she was his woman. It made me sick. And of course Lacey's ass wasn't too far behind. I don't know what dude she was with, but he was handsome. I hated these broads but one thing about them, they knew how to pick some good looking men. Snapping out of my thoughts, I waited until the hype died down a little before I made my way over to them.

Looking around, I was actually in awe. This bar was bigger than the first one he opened and the fact that I knew nothing about it, actually hurt my feelings. I was sure this bar would be making some good money too and to know I would be missing out on that, hurt me too. Rolling my eyes, I kept the tears from falling down my face.

Tre got up from the booth he was sitting in with everyone and I walked to where he was going. Carefully making my way past all of the people standing, I followed him to the back. The bathrooms were the other way so I didn't know what he was looking for, but as long as I got him alone, I could care less what it was. I stayed a good distance behind him so he wouldn't know that I was on his tail. Watching him slip into an office, I waited about a minute before I went in.

"Hey baby daddy," I greeted. He popped up startled, but regained his composure when he looked in my direction.

"Toya what are you doin' here?" He asked. And I got an

attitude. I couldn't believe that was the first thing that came out of his mouth when he saw me.

"We came to show our support," I said, rubbing my round belly. "You're not happy to see us?"

"Toya you gotta go man," he said in a dismissing tone. "We can talk later."

The fact that he was so dismissive had me pissed off and when I looked around him, I knew why. He had a few gifts sitting in the chair and I could only assume that they were for Averi.

"So this is why you want me out?" I snapped. "So you can give these stupid gifts to your new bitch?!"

"Watch ya mouth and it's none of your business what I do. If it has nothin' to do with our son, we don't have anything to talk about Toya. You don't get that?" His tone was so harsh and I can't believe it even came to this. I was about to say something, until the door to his office opened and Tre spoke before I could.

"Latoya can you go, please," he said with gritted teeth. Looking from him to Averi, I fought back the tears that were trying to come out of my eyes.

Looking to Averi again, she stood by the door in a nice tight bodycon romper that showed off her shape and she paired it with sneakers I have never even seen before. On another girl it probably would have looked basic as hell but Averi could pull anything off and it made me sick to my stomach.

"So this is it?" I asked, my tears falling. "This is really it?"

"I already told you if it isn't about the baby then we have nothin' to talk about." Averi walked around me and when she got to his desk, he put his arm around her waist and pulled her close.

The sight of the two of them made me sick and I couldn't watch it any longer. My head started to feel a little light and I felt like I would pass out. I started to waddle toward the door but the minute I took one step in that direction, I lost my footing a little and fell to the side. If Tre didn't have a case sitting up by the door, I would have fell right to the floor. Feeling his arms around me, he held me up and asked me if I was alright.

"I'm fine, let me go," I demanded, but he wouldn't let up.

"Go sit down," he said and tried to guide me to his desk, but I wasn't having it.

"Get off of me Tremaine!" I yelled. "I don't want to sit at the desk you probably had Averi laid out on! Leave me the fuc–" I tried to get out, but liquid gushing out of me and running down my leg stopped me from getting the rest of my words out.

"Fuck!" Tre yelled. "We need to get you to the hospital Toya." I would have objected, but the sharp pain that ripped through me made me scream out.

"It's too early Tre," I cried out. I knew I was in the safe zone to deliver, but I didn't want my son to come, not yet. Everything wasn't together and now I was regretting even bringing my ass to this grand opening.

"You're good Toya. Let's just get you to the hospital, now." I wanted to object but I knew I couldn't. Instead I let him guide me out of his office and out of the bar.

When the valet pulled his truck around, he helped me in and shut the door. I watched as Averi and his mom walked outside and they all shared a few words. His mom hugged him and gave him a kiss on the cheek and he hugged Averi tight and it lasted a little longer than it needed to. Beeping the horn at them, he jumped and ran around to the driver's side of the car. Putting the car in drive, we made our way to the hospital.

"PUSH!" The nurse yelled and if my legs weren't numb, I would have kicked her. "Push!" She yelled again and after that push, I was sure my son was out.

She pulled him out and hearing his cries, made me tear up but I didn't let one fall. They took him over to the table and Tre was about to follow, but I held his hand tight so he wouldn't go anywhere. Looking up at him, he had tears in his eyes and a Kool-Aid smile on his face. Seeing how happy he was tore at me and I knew when they brought my baby back to me, Tre's heart was going to be broken.

The nurse carried my baby over to me in a blue blanket and I was already in love with his little noises. She handed him to me and I looked down at him, but when I heard Tre behind me, that's where my attention was directed to.

"Tre, I-I c-c-an explain," I stuttered. The look in his eyes scared me and right now, I wanted to take my baby and dash for the door. I knew he wouldn't hurt my son, but there's no telling what he would do to me in this moment, regardless of me just giving birth.

"That's not my kid Toya?" He asked in the calmest tone. His voice was so low and calm it sent chills down my spine, I was too scared to answer him. But when he asked me again and raised his voice a little, I had no choice.

"No," I said putting my head down. I turned to face my baby even though he drifted off to sleep.

"So let me get this straight," he laughed sinisterly to himself. "You let me do all this shit for you, go to all of those appointments, spend all this time and money, and that's not even my baby you're holdin'?" Looking up at him, I was scared to answer him but I knew this day would come so I did.

"No Tre, it's not." I said sadly. I was hoping to get some kind of sympathy out of this situation, but I knew my chances of that were slim to none.

He stood by my side for a few more moments before he started flipping over everything that was in his way. All of the noise woke the baby up and the nurses that were in the room threatened to call security. Hearing that made him stop and before he walked out, he turned back and looked at me, his face showing nothing but hate and disgust. The door slammed and I watched him walk toward the exit. If Tre wasn't done with me before, he definitely was now.

I must have drove around Averi's apartment complex a million times, debating if I should ring her doorbell or not. It was well after two in the morning and I didn't want to wake her, but I didn't know where else to go. My mom called a few times to see what was going on, but I would fill her in on everything tomorrow. I knew she would give me a lecture and I didn't need that shit right now. I wanted comfort and I know Averi would be able to give me that.

Finally making the decision to go, I pulled into a guest parking space and hopped out. Walking up to the door and ringing the bell a few times, I didn't have to wait long before the light flipped on and she opened the door, looking flawless as usual.

"Tre? Are you alright? What's going on?" She rambled off question after question. I couldn't even answer her before I walked into her arms, breaking down in tears. She held me in her arms for a few minutes before she walked us inside and shut the door.

Guiding me over to the couch, she had me sit down and she took a seat right next to me. Picking my face up, she wiped my eyes and asked me if I wanted to talk. Shaking my head no, I told her all I wanted to do was lay here. She got up and we walked off to her room.

WAKING UP, it was almost nine and my head was pounding. I rolled over and Averi wasn't next to me anymore. I was ready to go find her, but the smell roaming through the house let me know that she was in the kitchen. A few moments later, she walked back in her room with a plate and juice in her hand.

"Here, you need to eat," she said, handing me the food. I loved Averi's cooking and I was actually starving. Scarfing down the food she made and downing the orange juice, I set the plate to the side and waited for her to lecture me.

"Why are you looking at me like that?" She laughed.

"Come on with it," I said. "I'm ready for the 'I told you so' and the lecture that I'm gonna hear from my mom too." Taking a seat next to me on the bed, she was about to speak but she smacked me in the back of the head, hard as hell. "The fuck was that for?"

"Being stupid," she said. "I'm not gonna lecture you because you're human; you fuck up from time to time. But that was stupid Tremaine and you know it was." I put my head down, but she picked it right back up.

"You'll be alright in due time," she assured. "I know you will and I'll be here every step of the way." I looked her in the eye and knew she meant every word. And before she was able to say anything else, I leaned over and kissed her.

I was a little surprised when she kissed me back, but I went with it and got more into it. Grabbing her face, I pulled her into me a little more and she straddled my lap. Pulling her shirt over her head, I tossed it to the side and attacked her neck. After a few more neck kisses, I worked my way back to her lips, my hands roaming all over her body.

Breaking away for a split second, Averi asked, "Are you sure we should do this? You just went–" she started, but I crashed my lips against hers again before she could finish.

Getting up, I flipped her over so that I was on top of her. She sat up so she could pull my shirt over my head and I leaned back down to attack her lips once more. Reaching below, I snatched her shorts down and pulled her under-wear to the side. Unbuckling and unbuttoning my jeans, I let them fall to the ground and slid my boxers down. Lowering myself, I slowly inserted myself in her and it felt so damn good.

"Shit," I moaned under my breath. Averi's moans in my ear had me excited and it brought me back to when we were in high school. I missed her, I missed this and I didn't want to lose any of it again.

Pulling my face up, I brought my lips to hers again and slammed into her a few times. A few more strokes like that and I released in her, falling to the side, both of us pant-ing. Sliding out of her, I walked to the bathroom and got us both a warm rag to clean up with. I let her put her clothes back on and I put my boxers on, laying back on the bed.

"What's on your mind?" I asked her when she finally laid down next to me.

"I-I'm not sure," she said.

"I know what's on mine." I looked to her and we made eye contact. "I love you Averi and I've never stopped loving you. I don't know what you want, but I know what I want and I want you. I need you. I don't care how long it takes or what it takes, but I need you Averi."

Looking at her, she had tears in her eyes and I scooted over to wipe them. I didn't know what was on her mind, but I was hoping it was at least something similar to what was on mine. It seemed like I waited forever for her to speak, but she finally gathered words after a few minutes.

"I love you too Tre," was all I needed to hear before I attacked her lips again, making her fall on her back. Moving her so she positioned under me, I spread her legs and put the cover over both of us to prepare for another round of some much needed making up.

WAKING UP AGAIN, it was going on two in the afternoon. Looking down, Averi laid on my chest looking so peaceful. I didn't want to move from this spot but I knew I had to go see my mom. When I checked my phone, there were so many missed calls and messages from her, even some from Latoya. I made a mental note to change my number tomorrow so I could rid of her ass for good.

Carefully peeling Averi's arms from around me, I slid out of the bed and went to the bathroom. After I freshened up in there, I walked back in the room and Averi was sitting up on the bed, looking edible.

"I didn't mean to wake you," I said apologetically.

"It's fine Tre," she replied laughing. "I needed to get up anyway, you know I can't sleep past eleven. I feel trifling." And we both shared a laugh.

"I gotta head up out of here though, need to go see ma," I said and she nodded her head. "You good? Need anything while I'm out? I'll come back." I started over to the side of the bed I slept on so I could put my sneakers on.

"No I'll be alright. Probably just gonna go to the gym and get a workout in or call Lacey up and do some work for this line. Are you okay?" I wanted to say no, but knowing Averi, she would worry about me more than herself and I wanted her to focus on what she had going on.

"I'm straight mama," I lied. "I'll hit you later though when I leave from dukes house, aight?" She nodded again and I walked to her side of the bed and kissed her a few times. Leaving out, I made sure to wait until she locked the door before I walked off to my truck.

When I got to my mom's house, I let myself in with my key and walked to the kitchen. I knew since it was Saturday she would be in here working on something to make and I was right when I noticed all of the utensils laid out on the table. She wasn't in the kitchen so I turned to go upstairs and as soon as I did, I felt the hardest smack to my face.

"The fuck was that for?" As soon as the words left my mouth I regretted it because she smacked the shit out of me again.

"Cuss in my house one more time Tremaine!" She yelled. Stepping around me, she walked in the kitchen and I already knew to follow. "Why haven't you been answering my damn calls?"

"Ma I'm sorry. I just wanted to be next to Averi last night." I expected her to yell again, but her face didn't change, except for the little smirk on her face. "Why you smirkin'?"

"Because after you didn't answer my calls, I called Averi. She told me you were fine and that you needed the night to get it together. But do that shit again, mama's gonna beat your ass like you're not grown, understand me?" I nodded my head like I was a little boy all over again. "Now tell me what happened."

I sat down at the table and told her everything. From the events last night up until this morning, leaving out the part about me and Averi crossing that line. I didn't know if I wanted to talk about me and Averi right now. I didn't know exactly how she felt. She said she loved me back, but it's always been like that. I didn't want to tell my mom something and then Averi tell her something else. I just hoped that eventually she would want the same thing as me.

I was sitting on the couch smoking my life away, stalking Averi's social media trying to find out where she's been or where's she's been staying. I was sick without her and I regret what I said to her that night, even though it was partially true. I fucked up forreal and I piss myself off every time I think about how I lost out on having a good woman and a good life. But I was going to try and get that back one way or another. I had to get Tre out of the picture first.

Forcing myself to get up, I went to the bathroom and got myself together so I could hopefully try and catch Averi today. I don't know if she switched her schedule around or not but when I tried to see her at work, her car was never there and when I went inside, she wasn't in the classroom. It pissed me off but I was hoping to find out where she was staying so I could pop up on her. Miami was a nice size, but she couldn't dodge me forever.

Hopping in my car, it was going on twelve, so I made my way to Lacey's house. Her car wasn't there when I pulled up and I wasn't trying to wait around, so I went to her little salon. The place was available the last time I drove around here, but a few times I tried to catch Averi over there, I saw Lacey walk in and out so I figured she got it. Pulling into a parking spot across the street, I waited for a few minutes to see if she showed. And when she pulled into a spot, I almost passed out. I prayed she would lead me to Averi today.

When she finally walked back out of the salon, she had her phone to her ear as she got in her car. It took her forever to pull off but when she finally did, I was right behind her. I didn't care if she was on the road for three hours at this point, as long as she got me to Averi. She made damn near a hundred stops, but then she finally drove into the direction of these nice apartments. If it wasn't where Averi was staying, I was bound to strangle her ass when she parked.

Following her around the complex, she finally pulled into a parking spot and I found a guest spot to pull into. It wasn't as close as I would have liked it to be, but I could still see everything I needed to. Watching her walk up to the door, she rang the bell and waited for about a minute until the door swung open and I laid eyes on my baby. She looked so beautiful and I couldn't wait to come back and get in her good graces. Making a mental note of where she stayed, I drove off to handle some other business.

Parking in the garage of the hospital, I checked my phone to see the room number Latoya gave me so I could drop in on her and the baby. Walking in the room, she and the baby were both gone, but I heard water running in the bathroom so I figured she was in there. Taking a seat in a chair by the window, I waited until she came out. And when she did I wished I stopped by sooner because her face was a bloody, bruised mess.

"The fuck happened to you?!" I asked, snapping. I wasn't her biggest fan right now because she couldn't keep her man away from Averi, but she didn't deserve this from whoever did it.

"I-I," she tried to get out but couldn't. She was hysterically crying and her lip was so busted and swollen, I didn't even want her talking right now.

"Do you have any ice?" I asked and she shook her head no. I got up to go out and get her something, but she stopped me and shook her head no again. Faster this time, like she was afraid of something.

"Toya, you need to tell me what happened," I said and this time it was more seriousness in my tone. I have never seen her so shaken up before and I knew it was serious if she looked like this.

Guiding her to the bed, I helped her sit back and get as comfortable as she could. Giving her the drink she asked for, she took a few sips and then broke down, telling me everything. She started with when she first got pregnant and telling me she was with someone else while she was with Tre and there was a high chance it was his baby. She finished with why her end of the plan couldn't be done and when she got to the part about why her face was beat up, I almost passed out.

"So whose baby is it Latoya?" My heart was beating out of my chest and I was praying like hell this wasn't my kid.

"It's y-yours Josiah." Shooting up off the bed, I started pacing around the room, my hands on my head.

This shit can't be happening, I thought. I fucked up. I fucked up bad. Me and Latoya took it there the day I picked Averi up from work, after I found out she was at Tre's mom's house. Averi thought that black car had something to do with work, but that was just Shad picking me up and taking me to Toya. That night we planned for me to propose to Averi, we had a few drinks and one thing led to another. I forgot all about it and never thought there was a possibility she could be carrying my baby.

Running my hands down my face, I let out a deep sigh. "Damn," was all I could get out. Babies are blessings, but this shit couldn't be happening, not when I'm trying to get Averi back. "Where is he?" I asked.

"With the nurses," she was speaking a little better, but I know it hurt for her to do that. "I could get him if you want to see him."

"Did they see your face already?" I asked. She nodded.

"I-I told them I d-didn't know or see who did it. That they came in at night and I woke up to this." She started crying and I went over to comfort her. What was supposed to be a cuss out and a quick trip, turned into a few hours of comforting.

The nurses ended up coming back to check on Toya I'm assuming and one was about to call security when she saw me sitting on the bed, but she assured them it was alright. The other nurse who stood by the door holding my son waited for the okay from Toya and then she brought him over to her.

"You want to see him?" She asked and I walked to the side of her, taking a look.

"He looks just like me," I said. He had a head full of curly black hair, his nose and his lips were shaped just like mine. He had Latoya's eyes, but my skin color, for right now. He was perfect.

"You want to hold him?" She asked.

I took a look down at my watch and it was getting late. I wanted to catch Averi, but at the same time I wanted to spend time with Latoya and my son. I felt bad for what happened to her and knowing that I had a son changed my perspective on some shit. I did want Averi back, but I would wait another day to get at her. Taking him from her hands, I walked back over to the chair I was sitting in and held him until I fell asleep.

LEAVING TOYA'S HOUSE, I got in the car to go get some things for the baby. She had been home for three weeks now and Julian was getting bigger by the day. His legs were so chunky and he stayed on Latoya's chest. When he was done feeding, she handed him to me and I went to go lay him down in his crib. Turning the monitor on and bringing the other piece with me, I jogged back downstairs.

"He went down easy?" She asked.

"Yeah, his little fat ass is knocked out," I laughed.

"Okay good," she smiled. "I need a shower. Just listen out for him, alright?"

"I got it, go shower musty." She threw a teddy bear at me but laughed as she went up the stairs.

Slipping my sneakers off, I leaned the recliner back and put my feet up. I had only been over here once while Tre was still living here, but she said they were all the way done and he hasn't been back here since the baby got home, so I was cool. After watching the sports channel for a few, I yelled for Latoya but she didn't answer so I figured she was sleeping. She definitely needed it and a nap didn't sound too bad while Juju was down for his. Leaning all the way back, I listened to the sports channel as I drifted off.

I don't know how long I was out for but I woke up to punch after punch. I didn't have much time to defend myself either; all I could do was put my head in my arms to block some of the hits. Getting thrown to the ground, I was kicked in the stomach and I was sure another one was about to follow, until I heard Averi's voice yelling for him to stop.

"Tre, stop! You did enough."

"Get the fuck up and out my house," he said. I was struggling a little but when I finally did, I looked at both him and Averi.

"Tremaine?" Latoya said when she got down the stairs. "What are you doin' over here? Get out," she demanded. I knew this shit wasn't going to end well and I wanted out.

"What am I doin' here? What's this nigga doin' in my house? The house that I paid for you to sleep in." He was pissed but I knew one thing, I would be ready if he tried to come at me again. This was the second time he got the best of me and I wasn't about to let it happen a third.

"H-he came by to—" she tried to speak, but was cut off by his yelling.

"He came by to what Toya?!"

"He came by to see his son!" She yelled. "And I'm not gonna feel bad about that shit Tre." Looking past him at Averi, I saw the look in her eyes and wished she didn't have to find out this way. I wish she didn't have to find out at all.

"That's true Jo?" Averi asked in that soft tone. I know her feelings were hurt but there's nothing I could do.

"Yeah," I admitted. "It's true and I'm so sorry."

"What are you apologizing to this bitch for Jo?" Latoya asked. It seemed as soon as the word bitch left her mouth, Averi was on her like white on rice. I never seen Averi in action, but I knew if she wasn't pulled off Latoya, she was bound to kill the girl.

"Alright Ave that's enough," Tre said, picking her off the floor. "You aight?" He asked and she nodded her head.

"If there wasn't a baby upstairs, I would make you figure out where you could lay your head. But as soon as this lease is up, good luck." And those were his last words before he walked out the door. Averi taking one last look at us with disgust, walked out right behind him, slamming the door and waking the baby up.

"So who's gonna get him?" I asked. If looks could kill, I would be one dead man. Latoya knew she would have to do it just in case she had to feed again. Slowly walking up the stairs, she went into his room and slammed the door.

"I'm gonna go to the crib and get some clothes!" I yelled up the stairs. "I'll be back in a little." She didn't reply, but I know she heard me. Walking outside, I made my way to the house.

Hopping out, I walked to unlock the door so I could pack a few things. My body was so sore and I couldn't wait to get back to her house and relax. I was just hoping she would get a lock change or something. I didn't need Tre popping up anytime he wanted, regardless of that being his house. Packing the last of my clothes, I slung the bag over my hurt shoulder and made my way out of the house.

As soon as I stepped outside, I wished I hadn't because I was knocked right back on my ass. And it didn't stop there. I was punched in the head repeatedly, kicked in the stomach and back and I was just ready for the Lord to take me right there. The hits stopped and I thought everybody walked away, but I knew I was wrong as soon as I heard a voice speak.

"Where's my fuckin' money," I heard. And right then I knew it was the dude me and Shad robbed one night.

"I-In the house," I stuttered. I thought I would get the chance to open the door, but it was kicked in and they all ran in to find it.

Not even a few minutes later, they all ran back out and then I heard tires screeching. Laying on the porch, I felt so stupid. I never thought I would get robbed, and when Averi left I didn't have to hide anything so I left the bag of money right on the floor in the closet. Now I was fucked up, broke, and had a kid. I didn't know what I was going to do right now, but I hoped Latoya was ready to take care of a nigga for a little while.

"He did what?!" Lacey yelled on the other end of the phone. After we left Tre's house, he dropped me off and I called her as soon as I got inside.

"He's been fuckin' around with Latoya this whole time Lace; they have a baby." I felt my voice crack and I didn't want to keep crying about it but I couldn't help it.

I never expected Josiah to cheat on me and with Latoya at that. This is the second time I got cheated on with her and I wanted to know what it was about her. And him having a baby with her, didn't make it any better. After telling Lacey everything else that happened, I broke down in tears.

"Stop crying Averi," she demanded. But I couldn't, mainly because my hormones were so out of whack.

"I'm fine," I said. "What are you doing today?" I walked off to the kitchen so I could make some tea.

"Malcolm is coming to pick me up in a little; are you going to be okay? I can stop by later if you want."

"No thanks, I'm just gonna sit on the couch and binge watch my show."

"Alright, I'll check on you later. I love you."

"I love you too," I replied and then we hung up. Putting the top on my tea, I grabbed a blanket out of the closet and sat on the couch, wrapped up and started watching Netflix. I wasn't into the show a good few minutes before my phone was ringing with a call from Tre.

"Hello," I answered.

"How you feelin'? You aight?" He asked.

"Yeah, just laying on the couch, watching my show."

"*Jane the Virgin?*" He asked.

"You know it," I replied, laughing. I'd just started watching it a couple of days ago and I was obsessed.

"You need anything while I'm out? I was gonna stop by the bars and then come check on you after." Some wings and fries did sound good right about now so I told him that he could bring that by when he was finished doing everything.

"Alright I'll be by soon," he said and then we hung up. I started playing my show, but the doorbell rang, making me pause it again.

I know Tre couldn't be here this fast, I thought. Walking to get it, I swung the door open and Josiah was on the other side looking horrible. I don't even know how he found out where I lived but he was about to go right back where he came from.

"What the hell are you doing here?"

"Averi I need your help right now," he said.

"Go ask Latoya," I replied. "Get off my doorstep Jo, I'm done with you." I tried to shut the door, but he put his foot in between.

"Averi," he said with more aggression. "I need your help, now. Can you let me in?" The look on his face went from calm to agitated and I didn't like the feeling I got from it.

"You need to go Josiah." I wasn't backing down, especially at my house. It was either him or me, and it definitely wasn't going to be me.

"Alright, have it your way," he said turning and limping away. I hurried to shut and lock the door then ran to get my pepper spray and taser.

When I went back into the living room, I looked out of the window and didn't see his car, so I figured he left. I walked to the couch, still clutching my spray and taser in my hand. Picking up my phone, I went to dial Tre.

"Wassup Ave? You aight?" He had worry in his tone, but I didn't want him rushing over, so I tried to speak as calmly as I could.

"Yeah, Josiah came by. He looked more beat up and said that he needs my help."

"What the fuck!" He screamed on the other end. "I'm on my way. Go upstairs and make sure you have your shit on you," he said.

Turning the television off, I hurriedly went up to my room. Closing and locking the door, I ran into the closet and locked the sliding doors.

"You in the back?" Tre asked and as soon as I answered,

I heard glass break downstairs and knew my window had been broken.

"He just broke in the house Tre," I said, getting kind of scared. But the feeling quickly went away when Tre assured me that I would be alright and he's coming to me.

"I love you Averi," he told me.

"I love you too Tremaine." Putting my phone to the side, I got ready for Josiah to come.

A couple minutes went by and I heard footsteps. Jo's feet were dragging since he was limping and I knew exactly where he was in the room.

"Come out Averi, I just wanna talk," he begged. "I'm sorry for everything baby, just come out and talk to me."

Scooting back in the closet a little more, I made sure my taser was out and I had a good grip on my pepper spray.

Hearing a knock on the closet door, my heart sped up in my chest but I held my composure.

"Averi I know you're in there," Jo said in a creepy tone. "I promise I just wanna talk. I need to explain." I kept quiet, knowing that Tre was speeding to get here and he was listening to everything.

"Dammit Averi!" He yelled, kicking at the door. "Open the damn doors, I told you all I wanna do is talk to you!"

The more he kicked at the bottom of the doors, the less they were holding on and I was ready for him to break through. He kicked a few more times before it stopped all together. I didn't know what happened, until I heard Lacey's voice asking where I was. Sliding the closet doors open, I ran out and hugged her.

"Are you okay?" She asked. Jo was laid out right next to the closet and I was glad.

"Yeah I'm good," I responded. "Thank you," I said to Malcolm.

"Ain't a thing," he said. "This is the same cat that robbed my lil' brother," he admitted. And I felt disgusted that this was the man I had been with. Putting my head down I started to cry, but Malcolm lifted my chin.

"Head up lil' mama." I looked at Lacey and she couldn't stop smiling.

"When did y'all even get here?" I asked. Taking another look at Jo's knocked out body, I kicked him in the stomach and watched him roll over.

"I told him I wanted to check on you before we went out and when I saw your window broken, I knew something wasn't right. He came straight up here and knocked Jo's ass out," she laughed.

I wanted to find the humor in this but I couldn't right now. To know that I really didn't know Jo like I thought, was scary. I was about to reply to her but Tre running in the room and planting his lips on mine, stopped me from saying anything.

"Averi baby, you okay?" He asked looking me up and down. I let out a small chuckle but I told him yes and he hugged me again.

"Okay Tre damn," Lacey said. "Before you suffocate her," she added.

"Fuck you Lacey," he told her and stuck his middle finger up at her. She stuck her tongue out at him and he waved her off. "But forreal Ave," he started. "You good?"

"Yes I'm okay," I said. "I just want his ass out of here." Tre and Malcolm nodded their heads at each other and dragged Jo out of the room.

Lacey looked back to make sure they were out of the room before she asked the question I was dreading. "So what's up with you and Tre?"

"Nothing," I said looking away from her. "We don't even know."

"Those red ass cheeks tell me otherwise," she said. "You're still feelin' him, aren't you?" Looking her in the eye, I knew there was no point in even trying to lie. She could read me like a book.

"I love him Lace," I admitted. "I shouldn't feel like this because I just called off the engagement with Jo not that long ago but I can't help how I've been feeling with all the time we've been spending together."

"You can't help how you feel Averi and Jo is a no good ass dude," she stated. "I've always told you that you can do better but for the sake of your happiness, I supported y'all. But enough is enough. You and Tre need to work this out because y'all both know wassup."

"I agree," Tre said, sneaking back in the room. The look on his face was all serious and I knew we were about to have a talk.

"I'm gonna go," Lacey said, backing away trying to be slick. "Babe, you ready?" She called down the steps. When Malcolm answered her, she gave me a hug and told me she would call and check on me later. Giving Tre a quick side hug, she raced down the stairs and I heard the door shut not long after.

"So where do we start?" I asked. Walking over to my bed, I sat and waited for the conversation that we should have had a long time ago.

"So where do we start?" Averi asked. I was ready to get deep into everything, but I wanted to make sure she was okay first. Especially after what she just went through.

"Making sure you're aight first," I followed her and sat next to her.

"I'm okay, Tre, I promise," she assured me. But I didn't believe all of that.

"It's okay if you're feelin' some type of way about that nigga Averi. You don't have to hide that."

"I'm not," she said. "I am upset that I feel like I don't know who I've been with for the past couple of years but I'm happy I seen him for who he really is. I needed that," she admitted. Nodding my head, I took in her words and spoke my peace, diving right into it.

"So where do you think that leaves us?" I asked, dreading her answer.

"I'll answer you, but I wanna know something first." And my heart was ready to jump out of my chest.

"Shoot," I replied.

"What was it about Latoya?" She asked and I knew it. "I mean, I got cheated on twice with her and you ended up with her after the fact. I just want to know what it is about her." She played with her fingers while she waited for the answer and I honestly didn't want to answer, but I knew I had to.

"She was easy at the time," I started off saying. "I was thinkin' with the wrong head when we were in high school and then you left me. To get over that, I just kept goin' back to her. Eventually she started tellin' everybody we were together and I went with the flow for so long, that it just ended up bein' that way." Taking a pause, I looked at her and she was all ears, so I kept going.

"The tables turned on me though; she cheated on me 'cause I wasn't makin' enough to satisfy her. And when my bar opened up, she came runnin' back all of a sudden but I should've seen through that. I took her back anyway. Then I started seeing how materialistic and shit she was and it just wasn't workin'. I stuck it out 'cause we went through a lot, but my heart wasn't in it after a while," I admitted.

Averi nodded her head, taking in everything I said. I hoped that didn't change anything between us. I wanted

Averi, needed her. And I would do just about anything to have us back again.

"It did hurt when I saw you two together," she said. "But I'm past it now. I can't deny my feelings have grown over the past few months either," she added, making me smile from ear to ear. "I just don't want to go through anything like that again."

"I promise you won't have to," I swore. I wasn't trying to shut her up or anything, but she made me the happiest man by saying those few words. "I love you Averi." And I meant that with every bone in my body.

"I love you too Tremaine." As soon as she said those words, I attacked her lips and pushed her back on the bed with my body.

Using my knee to spread her legs apart, I rested in between her legs, feeling her moist vagina through her shorts. Not breaking the kiss, I yanked at the strings of her tank, pulling it down to reveal her nice, plump breasts. Finally breaking away from her for a second, I took my shirt off and lifted her to take her tank off. I was about to resume the position we were in, but she stopped me.

"W-What's wrong?" I asked.

"I have to tell you something," she said. I got a little nervous, hoping that it wasn't anything bad. We just made things official and I didn't want anything ruining the moment.

"Averi you're scarin' me ma," I admitted truthfully.

"I'm pregnant," she said. And before I was able to get anything out, she interrupted. "It's yours before you get any ideas," she added. "I wouldn't do that and I haven't been with Josiah in months." Shutting her up by kissing her, I pushed her back down so I could finish what I started.

"Oh and another thing," I said breaking away from our kiss. "Don't ever in your life fight while you're carrying my baby. And you're movin' in with me." Nodding her head and smiling, she brought my lips back down to hers and I continued making love to the love of my life.

Fixing my tie in the mirror, Malcolm stood next to me.

"You ready for this bruh?" He asked and I shook my head up and down. Me and Malc became cool over the past few years. He and Lacey were going strong, they got engaged a month ago and are planning their wedding.

"As ready as I'll ever be," I replied. I couldn't believe I was marrying Averi today. It seemed like it was just yesterday we made it official and she told me she was pregnant. Eight months later, she gave birth to our beautiful baby girl Aviana and she was due to give birth to my son in another couple of months.

Finally putting the finishing touches on everything, I turned and my mom was walking in the room.

"My baby boy," she said, tears in her eyes. I wiped them as she laughed. "Didn't I tell you," she said. And I nodded. She always said to give it time and if it happened, it would. Now I was about to marry the love of my life.

"I'll be out there waiting," she said. Letting her walk out, I took one last look at myself before I dapped up Malcolm and followed him out the door.

Watching Averi walk down the aisle with her dad, I couldn't help but to shed a few tears. My soon-to-be wife looked so beautiful even under the veil, and I knew she was glowing from the pregnancy. When she stood in front of me, I shed a few more tears and she wiped them with her finger, with tears running down her face. As everyone took their seats and the officiant started to speak, I mouthed I love you to my wife and all I could think about was carrying her over the threshold of our new home.

"Do you Tremaine, take this woman Averi, to be your lawfully wedded wife, to have and to hold, in sickness and in health, in good times and woe, for richer or poorer, keeping yourself solely unto her for as long as you both shall live?" The officiant asked. "I do," I replied.

"Do you Averi, take this man Tremaine, to be your lawfully wedded husband, to have and to hold, in sickness and in health, in good times and woe, for richer or poorer, keeping yourself solely unto her for as long as you both shall live?" He repeated the same to her. "I do," she answered, tears rolling down her face.

"By the authority vested in me by the state of Florida I now pronounce you husband and wife. You may now kiss the bride." Giving me the green light to kiss my wife, I grabbed both sides of her face and brought her lips to mine.

Breaking away, I looked into her eyes and asked, "You promise to love me long time?"

"I promise husband," she said, making me the happiest man.

Walking hand in hand down the aisle, I was ready to get this woman home. After all the bullshit we went through, we finally came out on top, and together. Averi finally had her own studio for sessions and once she gave birth to our son, she was going back to work. I had both of my bars and I was working on a third business to open. The Jackson's were set and I was so ready to start this new journey with my wife. And I can't thank anyone but God for bringing her back into my life.

The End...

Text Shan to 22828 to stay up to date with new releases, sneak peeks, contest, and more....

SUBSCRIBE

Text Grand to 31996 to stay up to date with new releases, sneak peeks, contest, reading groups and more….

SUBMISSIONS

To submit your manuscript to Grand Penz Publications,
please send the first three chapters and synopsis to
grandpenzpublications@gmail.com

www.ingramcontent.com/pod-product-compliance
Lightning Source LLC
Chambersburg PA
CBHW061259120726
48001CB00001B/372